Red Lux.
OKAhCMPki"
406-4884

Sandy Kruse

MW00390284

The Mullett Boys

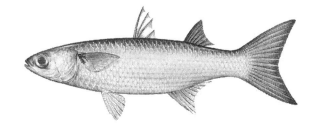

Red Fussell

Sandy Oard Kruse
Ruth McIntyre Williams

Published 2016
Barefoot Publications
Okahumpka, Florida

This is a work of total fiction with a twist. All the character names are friends of the author and a work of his imagination for the story. The locations, rivers and cities are their actual names and their locations. Even though the story is not a true story, this book depicts life's hardships on the river.

All Rights Reserved by James Carlton (Red) Fussell

Transcribed and edited by Sandy Oard Kruse
Edited and book design by Ruth McIntyre Williams

No part of this book may be reproduced or transmitted in any form or by any means, graphic, electronic, or mechanical, including photocopying, recording, taping, or by any information storage retrieval system, without permission in writing from the author.

List of Tales

The Mullett Boys

More Tales From the Withlacoochee River

Map of Towns and Areas

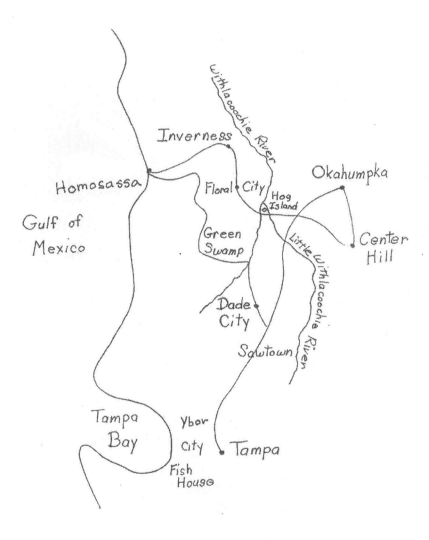

Descriptions of Areas

Sawtown – Area south of Dade City. During the big cypress days, the big sawmills brought in timber on the train. They'd lay track from the swamp to the sawmills and they'd snake the big timber out with big mules. They cut the timber with crosscut saws and axes. Some men jist sharpened the saws and put new handles in the axes. That's what my dad done.

This sawmill were in Sawtown. Sawtown ain't a town though. It's jist an area with the sawmill. The people that worked there lived there. Most worked 5 and a half days, and they paid a little fee for a place to sleep and git their meals. Most of the houses warn't all that good, but it kept the rain off, but not the skeeters. Malaria were bad in the swamps. The days was long and the nights was hot. It were very dangerous work 'cause trees could fall on them. Danger were everywhere.

At the sawmills, pay warn't much, but they had families that gotta eat and gotta have a place to stay. They was crooks all 'round, jist like today to rob and steal. The meals warn't all that good; jist beans, sow belly, hot coffee, cat-eye biskits, grits, eggs, and s'rup. The good cooks was big and fat.

The sawmills didn't pay in cash. They paid in tokens and we could only cash them at the commissary. They's a sayin', "I owe my soul to the company store."

The Green Swamp - The head water of the water shed for Central Florida starts here. The water flows north. So a spring starts water flowin' and into the Withlacoochee River. Clem worked for the railroad in the Green Swamp.

Hog Island – An island in Little Withlacoochee River. Water flows from Green Swamp.

About the Author

James Carlton Fussell, known to family and friends as "Red," was born in Okahumpka, Lake Country, Florida on October 11, 1932. He has lived in Okahumpka all his life, except for the years 1952 and 1953, when he served in South Korea as a corporal of the U. S. Army. He returned to Okahumpka and bought an auto repair shop, Guaranteed Muffler and Brake Shop, in nearby Leesburg.

He is married to Dorothy Fussell, also of Lake County, and has one married daughter, Carla, who lives in Kaleen, Texas. He has two grand-sons, Kyle, of San Diego, California, and Nicholas, of Kaleen Texas.

Preface

I wrote this here book. It's a made-up tale about hard times in Florida back in the late 1800s and early 1900s. How families dealt with it. Men had to work hard and make difficult decisions, jist to have food on the table for their families. It sometimes meant pickin' up and movin' somewhere else, like it done for us.

A bad winter 'bout took away our way to make a livin' in Okahumpka, so I'm gonna take y'all on the journey my family and I took to git to Homosassa where the winters warn't so hard. Y'all'll git to read 'bout my life as a 10 year old boy clear till the end.

In this-here book, I borrowed the names of my real-life friends I've met along the way, and used jist their names to create this fun story. The only truth to the book is the names of my friends and the towns mentioned throughout the book. But the life I've given all these friends in the book is total fiction at its best.

I think y'all'll enjoy the journey.

Red

The Big Move

Chapter 1

Times was hard in Center Hill, Florida. Lewis Fussell had 'bout all he could take. So he loaded 'is wagon and 'is wife, Ellie, two young boys, Lewis Jr. and Carlton. Carlton's me, but they call me Red. We was 'bout 10 and 12 years old. The year were 1891.

It were December and cold and rainy. The cold done kilt all the crops; our beans and our peas. We loaded all we had, which warn't much, but we did load the wood stove, beds, pots and pans, and the guns. Them guns was the important thangs.

We told Gramma we was goin' to Homosassa and fish for a livin'. The cold weather don't kill everythin' over on the Gulf like here in Center Hill. We had two mules, Pete and Kate. We tied the plow on the side of the wagon, and fixed the wagon with all the hay it would hold. The hay would keep us warm, and the mules would have food.

It were gettin' colder by the hour. We hoped to make it to the Withlacoochee River afore dark. We didn't think we'd have to wait for the man to take us over the river if'n we got there then. We went through Bushnell and was travelin' fast, but know'd we warn't gonna make it by dark. So we stopped at Hog Island on the riverbank of the Withlacoochee River.

It were 'bout dark when we got there. They was another family there too; they was goin' to Tampa and done left Ocoee 4 days ago. They had a big fire goin'. The man come out away from the fire and told us to come over by their fire. They was startin' to cook supper and sed they had plenty of food. They invited us to eat with 'em. We didn't want to put 'em out, but they insisted.

They had a young girl 'bout 8 years old. Lewis, Jr. sed she shore were purty. They cooked a big ole pot of beans and some cracklin' corn-bread. Mama dug out some of 'em sugar cookies and give everybody one. That girl thanked my mama with a hug 'round 'er neck. That shore made 'er feel good.

It were gettin' dark and time for bed. We give some hay to Pete and Kate and we laid in the hay wagon to keep warm. We had a blanket that Gramma made for us. She give my dad some money, but I don't know how much.

We got up as the sun come up, 'bout six. Dad started the fire. Them other people done left 'afore we got up. Dad cooked up some fatback bacon and made some of them cat-eye biskits and we had some cane s'rup. We'd save our breakfast to eat later, whilst we traveled.

We put the fire out; didn't wanna burn up the woods. We hitched up Pete and Kate and got on our way. Now we could eat our breakfast.

We was goin' the same way 'em other people was goin'.

Dad seen somethin' movin' up in the treeline and the sun were shi-nin' on somethin' bright. He thought it might be a gun. So we stopped and Dad pulled the mules behind some trees. He got out 'is shot gun and a handful of shells.

He told us, "Don't let 'em mules say nothin'." And he took off through the woods. We heard a shot, then another shot. Lewis, Jr. got 'is gun and put a bullet in it. We musta set there for 'bout an hour or more.

We seen Dad come back and asked 'im what happened. He jist sed, "Ain't none of y'all's business."

We come on down the road. Them people we met was loadin' their stuff back in their wagon. The man looked like somethin' hit 'im hard. My dad stopped to help 'im load 'is stuff. The woman come over to my mama cryin' and sed, "Two men beat my husband and was gonna rape me, but y'all's husband shot 'em."

Lewis and I helped Dad bury 'em in them trees out there. The wom-an sed, "Anythin' we have, y'all can have."

My mama sed, "Y'all already give me what I want–y'all's friendship."

The Mullet Boys

We loaded them up and we all left for the river. When we got there, my dad let' em go first, then the big boat come back to git us. When we got to the other side, we lost sight of 'em. Dad went to pay, but were told that man crossin' ahead of us done paid it.

The man with the big boat handed my dad a bag. He give it to my mama. She opened the bag and they was 2 gold dollars. I ain't never seen that much money afore, and my mama cried. I shore didn't understand that.

The Deer and the Bear

Chapter 2

Pete and Kate had one speed–slow, and the road were rough. We traveled 'bout 4 or 5 hours one day, when Lewis, Jr. raised 'is gun and fired. We stopped the wagon. He shot a couple of deer. They was two of 'em standin' there. So we got out of the wagon and walked where them deer was. My dad told Lewis, Jr. to gut both deer so they wouldn't spoil. Well, I hadn't shot 'em, but I knowed I'd have to gut one. Dad tied 'em on the back of the wagon.

We seen a house up the road, and we drove up in the wagon. The man come outside. My dad sed he'd killed 2 deer in 1 shot, and asked would they like one.

The man sed, "We shore would."

We asked if'n we could clean 'em there and he sed, "Y'all shore can." Then he asked where we was headin'.

We told 'im, "Homosassa, to fish."

He told us to bring them deer over, and we hung 'em up to skin 'em and cut the meat in strips. The man told my dad we could stay there a while and dry the meat so it would keep. And the man sed Lewis, Jr. were a real good hunter. After a bit he sed, "We got a bad bear in them woods. Do y'all think y'all's boy could kill 'im?"

My dad sed, "Shore he can; Lewis Jr.'s got a real good eye for huntin."

The Mullet Boys

So jist as the sun come up the next day, my dad sed. "Git up, boys. He wants that bear kilt." Now, we never shot a bear afore, but it would be like shootin' anythin' else, I guess. The bear were over in the river swamp.

We was plannin' on stayin' 'til the meat dried out, anyway.

Y'all had to be careful in them woods; y'all could git lost. So Lewis, Jr. got 'is rifle; it were a big ole gun. I had a shotgun; it had 2 barrels. I loaded that thang with buckshot.

We eased by the river and seen the bear's tracks. Lewis, Jr. sed, "Git in front. Y'all is better at trackin' than me." So we started through the swamp. It warn't long till I smelt 'im. I told Lewis, Jr. that he were in front of us. So Lewis, Jr., he gits in front. We was wadin' in water and mud, tryin' not to make no noise.

I seen Lewis, Jr. raise up and fire. He sed, "I think I got 'im." But I looked on my left and there another one stood up. I shot that one. I shot 'im with both barrels. He fell. I jist knowed I killed that bear. But I loaded my gun up again, jist in case he warn't kilt. I went out and

James Carlton Fussell

touched 'im with the gun. He were dead. We done kilt 2 bears.

I told Lewis, Jr. if'n he would gut 'em out, I'd go get the mule to take 'em back. But Lewis, Jr. didn't wanna do that. So I gutted both bears. It didn't take me very long. I used the knife my dad made for me in 'is blacksmith shop back in Center Hill; it were real sharp.

I were sittin' on a stump waitin' for Lewis to come back when here come an old hog. He smelt 'em bear guts. I raised the gun up, but that hog heard me and run. I looked to the right; there was my dad with the man where we was stayin'. They picked up one of 'em bears to put on the mule, but that mule kicked and took off runnin' through them woods. He were headin' to the barn. He didn't want nothin' to do with that there bear. It were funny to watch 'im take off runnin'.

So the men went back and got the wagon and hitched up the ole wore-out mule. He didn't like it, but he were too old to run. We got back to the man's house, skinned them bear and cut 'em up to dry out.

The man tried to git my dad to stay there, but he sed. "We's goin' fishin'." My dad told 'im he could sharpen axes and cross cut saws too. The man told my dad that Big Cypress in Sawtown shore needed somebody to sharpen saws, axes and cross cut saws. They paid a good 2 dollars a day. He sed, "And they'll give y'all a place to stay and food to eat."

We stayed with that man and 'is family jist over a week. The meat done dried out, so we was gonna leave one whole bear with them. Dad sed, "Boys, we need to be goin'. Y'all clean up the barn. Shovel out the cow and horse poop, feed all them animals, and then we'll leave when the work's done. We'll be leavin' in the mornin' at first light."

The man's wife and girls begged my dad to stay. The man even promised he'd give my dad a farm of 'is own. But we jist had to go on to Homosassa. Afore we left, the man give me one of 'is new guns that shot shells. He give Lewis, Jr. a pistol that shot .22 shells. His wife fixed a bunch of food and brought out a box of stuff we done left in the house.

We hadn't come very far, no more'n 30 miles in total, and we'd already been gone three whole weeks. We had plenty of food to last a while, but the first time we et any of the bear meat, I learned the bear we took with us were so tuff it would take me all day to chew it. I'm jist shore that were the bear my brother kilt.

The next day, they were a light rain, but it done warmed up. That night we camped on a small lake. My mama looked in the box the lady give 'er, and there were a silk tablecloth. She were so happy it made all of us happy.

My dad sed, "Boys, we don't know this part of the country, so y'all need to stay awake and guard what we have. Y'all can sleep when we travel." My dad built a big fire, but told us not to set by it. If'n someone were gonna rob us, they'd shoot all them next to the fire. So we hid under the wagon, but oh my, that fire shore felt good.

Nothin' had been 'round and we was jist 'bout asleep, when I shook my brother. They were a man there and 2 more at the edge of the woods, comin' our way. We could see 'em from the light of the fire. Lewis, Jr. raised that pistol and shot at one in the woods. I heard 'im holler, so I knowed he'd been hit. Then he shot at the one at the back of the wagon and hit 'im in the foot. He shot the third one in the rear end. All 3 of them hollered real good. They knowed they'd been hit, and they all 3 headed into the forest.

Dad wanted to know what were goin' on. Lewis, Jr. told 'im they was gonna rob us, but he hit 3 of 'em. My dad sed, "We might jist as well git up and go on."

We got to Floral City 'bout daylight. One store were jist openin' 'is doors. We stopped to make shore we was goin' the right way, and told the man in the store 'bout them robbers.

He told us, "That bunch is bad, so y'all better watch real good. They's jist as soon shoot y'all as look at y'all. No tellin' how many people they's kilt. Everybody 'round here's 'fraid of 'em boys, even the law." They's 'bout 5 of 'em boys. They steal cows. People's all 'fraid to do nothin.'"

We started out again and promised to watch out for 'em. It started to rain a little bit. The road were bad and rough. We'd been gone 'bout 4 hours and my dad stopped and sed, "Boys, look up there in the edge of the woods. Lewis, Jr., git y'all's gun and come with me." I asked if'n I could go, but Dad sed, "No, get off the wagon and build a fire like y'all was gonna cook. Then slip through the woods." So I built a good fire. My mama laid there with my gun in case they come at the wagon.

'Bout 30 minutes to an hour later them men hadn't made no noise, but we could still see 'em in the edge of the woods. Then I heard 2 shots. Dad and Lewis got 2 of them men.

I looked up and here come one of 'em crooks ridin' from the woods to the road and right at our wagon. He got all that horse would give 'im. Then there were another shot; that horse were still comin', but the rider were gone. My mama done knocked 'im clean out of the saddle. I never knowed she could shoot like that.

I hurried back from the wooded area and caught the horse; he were purty scared with all that shootin' goin' on. I finally got 'im calmed down. My dad and Lewis, Jr. both come back from the woods to the wagon. They got the shovel to bury them dead men. Lewis Jr. sed, "The man I shot in the foot, well, 'is foot looked purty bad. It were all swelled up."

Dad dug 3 deep holes in them woods. We buried the men and covered the holes with leaves, and then we got all the blood off the road where Mama kilt that man. We didn't want nobody to know what we'd done.

Dad tied the horses to the back of the wagon. It were gettin' dark, so 'bout 5 miles down the road, we took them horses through the woods to a pond. We took the saddles off them horses and throwed the saddles in the pond. They sunk in 'bout 4 foot of water.

My dad sed, "Go git me 3 pine cones." I didn't know what for, but he told me to do it, so I done it. He took the halter off and put the pine cone under the horses' tails, whacked 'em on the hind quarter and headed 'em west. They kicked with both feet and took off runnin' as fast as they could go.

We was still goin' west. He sed we had 'bout 2 more days and we would be there, if'n no body bothered us. They was crooks all over them woods, and we wasn't gonna let 'em have none of our stuff.

The Storm

Chapter 3

We traveled all night long, through the horse stuff in the woods and was down the road when daylight broke. The sky shore looked bad. My dad seen a horse barn and we went up there. The man come out on the porch. My dad asked if'n we could go in 'is barn to get out of the weather.

He sed, "Shore thang. The weather looks real bad. Let me open the barn door."

It warn't very clean, like what we was used to. The man sed, "Y'all come in the house when y'all get settled down."

My dad told 'im that Lewis, Jr. and I, we'd stay in the barn. The storm looked real bad. We unhitched Pete and Kate and give 'em some feed and rubbed 'em down. They shore liked that. They had 3 mules, good size, so we fed 'em and wiped 'em down, too. We put the hay all in one place and pulled all the poop out of the stalls into the walkway. We got some corn and pumped the trough full of water to give to Pete and Kate. We didn't think he'd mind.

We finally got all the cow and horse poop clear out of the barn and over by the fence, hung up the tack, chain and collars. We left the barn purty clean.

They sed to come in for supper. The woman done cooked up a big

James Carlton Fussell

ole pot of turtle soup and made some cracklin' cornbread. She give Lewis, Jr. and me a cup of hot chocolate. That were the first hot chocolate I ever did drink, and it shore were good.

Crakling Corn bread

1/2 c water ground meal

1/2 Tbsp Lard

1/2 c floor

1 Egg

milk enought To mix

1 c cracking

On hog Killing DAY Cook All The Lard out the hog skin. Then Sqeze out all The Lard you can. Then dry In The sun. Then TAKe A floor sAck put the skin in sAck beat it with a hammer Till it Broke in small peaces The mix with the Corn bread Cook for 20 mints At 350 degeiss

The wind were blowin' hard. We was glad we warn't on the Gulf with that wind blowin' 'bout 100 miles an hour in this bad storm. We et and was goin' back to the barn, but they sed we should stay in the house. We told 'em we had to look after Pete and Kate. So they told us to jist be careful. It were hard to walk 'cause of the wind, and the rain hurt when it hit our faces. We got back to the barn and went up in the hay loft. We took off our wet pants and shirts and rolled up in our blankets to sleep for the night.

When we woke up the next mornin' the wind were still blowin' jist as hard. And them pants was still wet, but they would dry out. We fed Pete and Kate and then fed the man's horses and milked 'is cow and fed 'is chickens.

Their ole rooster were crazy. He crowed all night long; maybe he were scared. Afore we milked the cow we washed 'er down good like Mama told us to. We took the bucket of milk to the house and got a little wet, but we didn't care. The man who lived there sed he needed to go feed 'is stock, but we told 'im we already done that. So we et breakfast. It were real good; grits, eggs, fatback bacon, cat eye biskits, with some of that guava jelly.

Dad let us have a cup of coffee. Whew Doggie! It were strong. We thanked the lady for somethin' to eat.

The wind were still blowin' hard when we went back to the barn. We cleaned everythin' we could. One of 'em gates was bad, so Lewis, Jr. fixed it. We put all the tools where it looked like they needed to be. It shore looked better when we got it all cleaned up. We climbed up in the hay.

I sed, "Lewis, I'd shore like to know if'n them men we kilt had kids."

But he sed, "Bet if'n they did, they's jist like 'em."

We heard a noise and looked down. It were the man who owned the barn. He hollered, "Hey, boys."

We sed, "We's up here."

We climbed down the ladder and he sed, "It shore looks good out here. It ain't looked this good for many years." Then he told us they had a son, and a bunch of crooks kilt 'im.

"That wild bunch in Inverness done it, and they's still a bunch of 'em 'round. Everybody's scared of 'em, so nobody does nothin' 'bout it." Lewis, Jr. give me the quiet sign. Now I were real glad they was in the grave.

The wind blowed 'bout 3 days afore it let up. My dad sed it were time to go. I liked it here, but I knowed we gotta go on to Homosassa. It done rained a lot and the road were muddy. It shore would be hard on Pete and Kate. Dad asked the man if'n he could leave most of our stuff in 'is barn for a bit so the wagon wouldn't be so heavy in the mud.

He sed, "Shore."

So we left all our stuff in the barn, where we'd cleaned it. We only got 'bout 4 miles to go. We took the gun, saws, axes, pots and pans with us. It shore were gonna be hard goin' at first, but we still took 'em.

The Sheriff

Chapter 4

We left and the sun were shinin'. It looked like it were gonna be a nice day. We'd gone 'bout 3 hours when 2 riders come up and wanted to know if'n we seen 3 men on horseback in the last week. We sed, "No, we been in a man's barn while it stormed." We asked what they wanted the men for, and they sed they thought somebody kilt 'em, 'cause they ain't seen 'em for at least a week.

I thought, *Can't see 'em when they's in the ground where they belong.*

He sed, "I found their horses 'bout 40 miles from here. Guess I'll jist keep 'em."

We asked, "Are y'all the sheriff?"

He sed, "Yes."

My dad asked, "Could I buy 'em horses, if'n y'all don't find who owns them? I'll keep them."

Sheriff sed, "Where y'all headed?"

We sed, "We're goin' to Homosassa to fish."

The sheriff sed, "That's the best way I know to starve to death. Them fishermen, none of 'em have nothin' but an ole wore out boat and a wife with kids. As soon as them kids get big enough, they leave for Tampa to work in the shipyard. Y'all gonna farm?"

Dad sed, "If'n I have to, but I'm a blacksmith. I can make 'bout anythin.'"

Sheriff sed, "The closest blacksmith be in Inverness. That's a good ways. I could use one ever once in a while. Let me know when y'all set up. I gotta be on my way.

See y'all later."

The Miller Place

Chapter 5

I looked on the right side of the road there, and seen a blue hole of water. It were a spring, and I could see fish in it!

Then we got on a real bad road. It were lined with trees makin' a roof, but it were a real rough road. My mama sed it were hard on 'er behind. But my dad told 'er it'd be jist a little bit 'til we'd git there.

We come to a shack. It looked purty bad, but my dad sed, "This is it."

I thought, *Even a hog wouldn't stay here!* An ole man were walkin' down the road. Dad asked 'im if'n this were the Miller place.

He sed, "Shore is. Y'all gonna live there? Them skeeters will tote y'all off."

My dad sed, "Y'all live 'round here?'

"Shore do. Been here afore the Indian War. Them Indians burned everthin' we had, kilt my boy and my wife."

We got out of the wagon to look around. I walked down by the ditch and seen a big ole snake. I sed, "Lewis, shoot that snake."

But the ole man sed, "No, don't shoot that there snake. It's a good snake. That there's a blue racer, so it keeps all them bad snakes away. Let 'im be."

Guess we gotta learn what's good and what's bad 'round here. We walked into the shack. It weren't all that bad. We went to work on it

James Carlton Fussell

and started cleanin' it up. One of the neighbors down the road 'bout a mile or more sed, "Y'all need to smoke it."

We sed, "How do y'all do that?"

Sed, "Put rags in a bucket and burn 'em. That gits rid of snakes and spiders and all kind of bugs. Them burnt rags don't smell good and it kills some of 'em bugs."

So I go git the stuff to do it with. We smoked our house. He were right. It don't smell very good, but 'em bugs was gone. They's a wood stove. It looked better than my mama's. The kitchen were small, but it would do. The place had 2 bedrooms. They's both small, and then they's a real small room that Lewis, Jr. got. All's we gonna do were sleep in there. They were an ole bed, and it looked purty bad. They's a fire place. It looked good, made of rock. I bet it burned lots of wood. They were a pitcher pump in the kitchen and a place to wash dishes. It were made of wood, but looked good. The water jist run out on the ground.

They was an oil lamp, but we didn't have no oil. The ole man sed he got some. It were a nickel a gallon. So Dad paid 'im the nickel.

We was tired, so Dad helped Lewis and me git some hay out of the wagon; put it on all the bed springs, and we all laid down in our beds and went to sleep. I'd jist gone to sleep when it were daylight and time to git up. I were ready to go fishin', but that would be a while. We had to clean up this place first. My mama wouldn't stand for a trashy place. First, we cleaned, and burned wood, and put the rest of the trash in the ditch. We'll fill it up and put dirt on it to make a big yard. We worked all day long. Mama helped, too, and it looked purty good.

Lewis, Jr. cleaned the roof and got all them limbs off. They was some holes in the roof, so the next day he fixed the roof and we cleaned more of the yard. We looked down the road and they was some people comin' our way. They sed they come to help clean it up. They knowed Mr. Miller didn't clean much.

'Bout noon my dad went back to git what we'd left in the barn 'bout 4 miles up the road. When he got back he told Lewis, Jr., "That man, where we stayed, made a boat, and sed we could have it. Y'all can go git it when the work's all done here." Then 2 days later it were all done, with them people's help.

I asked one of the men if'n he would teach me to fish. The man sed, "If'n y'all think y'all're gonna make a livin' fishin', y'all will starve to death. All of us have other jobs. Fishin' is hard work with very little pay. I hear y'all's dad's a blacksmith. We need one of 'em 'round here. Y'all should learn that. I'll teach y'all how to fish, but I keep the fish."

Goin' Fishin'

Chapter 6

The man come by and told me to be ready in the mornin' 'bout 4:30 and we'd go fishin'. I sed I'd be there. I told my mama I were goin' fishin' in the mornin' and she sed, "Okay."

I were there at 'is boat at 4:30; it warn't a very big boat. He'd git on one side and I'd git on the other side. We had to do it that way so the boat would go straight. We went for 'bout an hour in the Gulf. He sed, "Don't go left there. They's rock."

I never knowed they was rock in the Gulf. He throwed in a lead weight on the hook, then pulled it up and looked at the bottom of the weight. He done it again. I thought, *Them fish ain't gonna bite that*. So he pulled the anchor out and let the boat drift back so we'd be right on the rock bed. That lead weight were what he used so he'd know when we was on the rock bed.

He handed me a pole with a big hook on it, and put a piece of fatback bacon on it. He sed, "Y'all don't need no cork."

I dropped it in the water and caught a fish that were jist 'bout all I could handle. I got 'im to the boat and the man took a stick with a hook on it and snatched that there fish into the boat.

He sed, "Now take that hook out, but don't let 'em bite y'all." It were a big fish. We caught 'bout 20 fish in all.

I sed, "How much did y'all make?"

He sed, "'Bout 3 dollars. Mullet's cheap fish. You git 'bout 5 cents a pound."

So we started rowin' back to the river. He told me to git out of sight or them in that fancy boat out on the Gulf would shoot us. They were a war goin' on out there. I don't know what it were, but they's shootin' at each other. I seen a dead man that done got shot floatin' by the boat. I jist let the crabs have 'im. I shore didn't wanna git shot. They had a fast boat. The man sed they had a motor on it.

I sed, "What's a motor?" He told me that's what makes the boat go fast. So after they passed us, we got our boat back to the dock.

A woman come down to buy fish. She wanted a small one, so he sold it to 'er for 50 cents, but he give 'er a big one. She's got 5 kids. She really did need a big one. He sed, "Some people need more than others, so never be greedy. You may need somethin' some day."

I started to leave. I thanked 'im for takin' me fishin' and he sed, "Take one of them fish."

I looked at 'em and told 'im, "I jist need one for 4 of us."

But he handed me a big ole fish. I sed, "No, it's too big. Jist gimmee a small one." So he handed me one that would do.

"Y'all ever cleaned a fish?"

Sed, "No."

He sed, "I'll show y'all jist one time. Then y'all're on y'all's own."

He cleaned it so quick I still didn't hardly even know how. I took the fish home and give it to my mama. She fried it in cornmeal that Dad ground back in Center Hill at Cason Station, near Okahumpka. She fried 'im up, and cooked some of 'em pokeberry leaves up, and made some hush puppies. If'n it got better'n that, I don't know what I would do.

Lewis, Jr. and my dad left to git the boat the man give us. They'd git them crab traps too. I ain't never et no crab, but I'm shore gonna. They had to fix the boat, but it looked good. He give Lewis, Jr. some paint to paint it and sed, "Put y'all's name on them big balls on the crab traps too."

When my brother seen the fish cooked up and 'em pokeberry leaves, he sed, "Whew Doggie! We gonna eat tonight!"

Them fish was good and 'em greens too. I were full.

James Carlton Fussell

pokeberry

1/4 Lb salt pork
1 1/2 Lb Tender pokeberry Leaf
3 qt cold water

place salt pork in cold water
bring To A boil uncovered make sure
you have only Tender leaves Then
bruised The Leaves Them ad To
The pot cook for 1 hour salt And pepper

Pokeberries

The Outhouse

Chapter 7

My dad sed, "Tomorrow we gotta build an outhouse. See if y'all can scrape up some lumber." So that mornin' I went over to the fisherman's house and told 'im what we needed.

He sed, "They's an ole house over by the river. I'll help y'all go git some wood. So we took 'is boat to git a boatload of good lumber to build the outhouse, but not too close to our house.

We built a two-holer and put a door on it. My dad made a moon and put it on the door. A moon meant it were for women. And he used a board on the top.

"We gotta go git some tin somewhere to cover the top, so it don't leak when it rains."

The next day I asked the man with the boat if'n he would take me back to that house by the river to look for some tin.

He sed, "Shore."

We left and went back to that same house. We found jist enough tin to cover the whole top of our outhouse. Now we won't get wet if'n it rains and we're in there.

James Carlton Fussell

This outhouse was built by the WPA in the 1930s, and is still in use today
on Red's property. The door opens on the right.
(photo by Sandy Oard Kruse)

Loss of a Friend

Chapter 8

The winter looked good. I walked over to my fishin' friend's house. His wife told me that he were sick. I seen 'is boat had water in it, so I got me a can and dipped the water out. It were leakin' in a crack.

I asked my dad how to fix it. He got some tar and a rag. He'd already made a tool to fix Lewis, Jr.'s boat, so he brought it over and patched the fisherman's boat. They was two sheds where the fisherman kept 'is boat, and the man let Lewis put 'is boat in there, too. That way when it rained it wouldn't sink.

I stopped by to see the man again, but he were still sick. And I noticed on the shelves where they put their food, they warn't none. They tell y'all in the swamp, goin' to the right, they's deer in there. So I asked Lewis, Jr. if'n he wanted to go huntin'.

And he sed, "Why not?"

We left the next mornin' and waded through the swamp. 'Bout noon Lewis shot. "I got one!" he sed.

We gutted it out and carried it out of the woods. We was lookin' at the Gulf, then seen one of 'em fancy boats with a motor out in the Gulf. I told Lewis that we needed to hide, and he wanted to know why. Then we seen another boat. One was chasin' the other. They was shootin' at each other so we hid. The one boat were goin' 'round and 'round.

James Carlton Fussell

The other boat come up and stopped the boat. They threw some-thin' out of the boat, and they dragged the boat away.

We got our deer and went through the swamp to the house. Dad done made a smoker. I told 'im 'bout the fisherman bein' sick and I wanted to smoke the deer to give to 'im. We could keep some, but not much. Dad jist sed, "Y'all gotta do the smokin'."

So I go git the hickory limbs and leaves and git my fire goin'. I skinned the deer and cut it in strips. It were 2 days that I had to smoke it. We kept some, and I took the rest down to the fisherman's house and knocked on the door. His wife come to the door and I give 'er the deer. She looked at me and cried. My mama give 'er some stuff too. I didn't know why, but she hugged me and thanked me. I left and thought, *At least they got somethin' to eat.*

I come back home and got me a piece of backstrap. It shore were good.

It were startin' to rain real hard. My mama sed, "Git out of the rain afore y'all catch a bad cold." So I went inside the house by the wood stove. It shore felt good. My brother come inside and he were all wet. My mama sed, "What happened to y'all?"

He sed, "I fell off the dock."

I laughed.

And he sed, "It ain't funny. That water's cold! They's somethin' goin' on at the fisherman's house. They's a whole bunch of people down there."

I sed, "I were jist down there not long ago and give 'em that deer y'all kilt."

When my dad opened the wood shutter to see what were goin' on, he sed, "I'll go see."

He were gone jist a little while. When he come back he sed, "The fisherman died and 'is wife shore is upset."

Dad were gonna see if'n they wanted 'im to make a box to put the fisherman in. So when he come back he went out to where we kept the lumber. He told me to go fire up the forge to make some nails. I knowed how to make 'em. My brother helped 'im get the lumber, and in a while they started buildin' the box.

I got the forge goin' and it were gittin' real hot. It had to be 2000 degrees to work good. I had the blower goin' when up walked one of 'em boys that lived down the road. I told 'im to turn the thang for me, and he done it. It got hot real quick. I made small nails; they make up real quick and that's what he wanted. When I made one I dropped it in the water; that made it hard. When I thought I had enough I took 'em to Dad. They was jist what he wanted, and he made the box.

My mama walked out with that silk table cloth and he put it in the box. I know'd she wanted to keep it, but like that fisherman sed, "Never be greedy." That's what she were doin'. I wanted to tell 'er to keep it, but knowed she wouldn't.

They was 2 men down at the graveyard diggin' a hole to put 'im in. The weather were hot so the fisherman would start to smell bad soon. The box were made, and it sure looked good. Dad does real good work.

They took the box down to put the fisherman in it, but 'is wife seen the silk table cloth and told my mama she should keep it, 'cause it's where it belonged. They put 'im in the box, and then put 'im on the kitchen table. She sed, "We'll bury 'im on Saturday." That would be quick.

Whilst we was walkin' home my dad told me to go make 'im a head stone. I sed, "I don't know how."

He sed, "I'll show y'all. Git a good flat rock and build a hot fire. Put the rock in the fire 'til the rock gits good an' hot."

I sed, "I don't even know 'is name."

But Dad sed, "I know. It's Ray Emerson. He's lived here all 'is life. He were forty years old and don't have no kids. Loved to fish."

Then he got some cool water and fixed a cup to put a small amount on the rock. When he put the water on it, he made the letters. He couldn't read, but my mama wrote it out for 'im. It looked purty good.

The next day they put the fisherman in a wagon, and took 'im to the graveyard and put 'im in the hole. Then one of them men read from the Bible. They sed their goodbyes and they all went to the fisherman's house. They took food and water to drink, but didn't stay long. We all went home. I told my mama that I shore would miss 'im and I was still gonna learn to fish.

The next day the fisherman's wife knocked on our door. She seen me and sed, "I'm gonna give y'all the boat and the house, and I'm gonna go live with my mother. I don't need this place no more. I never did like it."

I sed, "I can't pay y'all for it."

She sed, "Here's the deed for the boat and the house and everythin'. I jist want one thang, would y'all take me to the stage line?"

I sed, "Y'all don't have to give me nothin', but I'll still take y'all to the stage line."

But she jist sed, "Thank y'all, but I don't want none of this no more; this place is y'alls."

So Dad hitched up Kate and Pete and had me take 'er to the stage line. We left 'bout 8 in the mornin' to git to the stage line. It would be a little while afore the stage would come. Whilst we was waitin', 2 riders come down the road. I didn't like their looks, but I had Lewis, Jr.'s 22 pistol, and I had it by my side. I looked up and there come the sheriff. Them riders rode off. The sheriff jist stopped to say, "Hi."

When the fisherman's wife started to git off the wagon, I sed, "My mama told me to give y'all this." It were one of them gold dollars.

She sed, "I can't take it, but y'all 'member, never be greedy."

That's what the fisherman told me, too. I liked 'im. I turned the wagon 'round and headed home. I knowed I'd have 'bout an hour afore I'd git home. I turned onto the road to go home, and there was 'em bad-lookin' men. One of 'em sed, "Y'all got any money, boy?"

Sed, "No, sir, I don't."

They sed, "Well, we might just take the mules."

I thought, *Oh no, not Kate and Pete!*

He got off 'is horse and come toward me. I took that .22 and shot 'is hat off. The other guy went for 'is gun, so I shot 'im in 'is foot. He hol-

done it."

He asked why I shot 'em, and I told 'im 'cause they was gonna rob me.

When the sheriff tried to talk to 'em, one pulled 'is gun and fired. Somehow the barrel had a stick in it and it blowed 'is hand off. The sheriff shot both of them. They was some of that bad bunch from Inverness. They never did find them other 3, but the sheriff still had their horses.

He sed he had to leave and told us, "See y'all later."

I were glad he were gone and sed, "Let's go look at the boat. It shore looks good, but I wish the fisherman were still here." Then I told Lewis, Jr., "Let's set 'em crab traps."

But he sed, "We ain't got no bait for the traps."

Well, I'd seen a cast net by the boat, but I didn't know how to cast it.

I asked 'round if anybody knowed how to cast it, and they sed ole man Jones' boy could throw it. I asked where he lived, and learned it were jist a mite down the road.

Learnin' to Throw a Cast Net

Chapter 10

I took Kate and rode 'er to ole man Jones' house. I knocked on the door and Mr. Jones sed, "The door's open. Come on in." I walked in, and he were sittin' in 'is chair. They was 3 young girls in there, too.

I sed, "I need some help."

He asked, "What kind of help do y'all need?"

So I explained that I needed to learn how to throw a cast net.

One of 'em girls got up and sed, "I'll teach y'all."

So I asked how much it would cost me, and they jist laughed. She sed, "If'n y'all let me fish too, I'll do it for nothin'. Do y'all know how to fish?"

I sed, "No."

And they all laughed again.

She sed. "I'm one of the best fishermen 'round here. Why don't we go in the mornin' in my boat, and we'll go where we can catch fish with the cast net."

I told 'er that would be fine, and she sed she would have the boat ready 'bout 5:30.

She showed up 'bout 5:30. I ain't never seen a girl with pants on afore. We pushed the boat from the bank. She'd git on one side and I'd git on the other. We started on through Hell's Gate, turned left, then 2 right turns, then 2 left turns and back right. Whew doggie! Them rocks is bad here, but we got through. We was on the Gulf.

I asked 'er what 'er name were, and she sed, "Sam." Well, I thought that were a boy's name, but didn't say nothin'.

She sed, "I know y'all's name. It's Red."

Sam casting a net in the early morning.

I didn't like it that she knowed my name and I didn't know hers, but I let it go. She got the pot out to put the fish in when we catch 'em, and we put out the anchor. We net fished 'til 'bout noon and she sed, "Let's eat."

Well, I ain't brought nothin' to eat, jist some water. But she handed me a big ole piece of somethin'. I ain't sure what it were, but it were good. While we et I asked 'er where 'er brother were.

She sed, "We ain't got no brother. Jist us girls."

James Carlton Fussell

We caught 'bout 40 fish, some big, some small. She caught 35 of 'em. I liked 'er.

She fished smart. We was on the boat back to the river when we seen them boats chasin' each other.

She sed, "Let's hide." We poled the boat into the trees so they couldn't see us, and we was sittin' real still. They went by real close, but they didn't see us. They went on by and then she sed, "I ain't never been kissed."

Well, I ain't neither. So I kissed 'er and she sed she liked it. She sed, "That'll be my pay."

But I sed, "No, we split what we git." So she kissed me. And I liked it, too.

We went on back down to the landin' and there were that ole woman standin' at the dock for a fish. She wanted a small one, but she's got that bunch of kids to feed. Sam sed, "When that ole woman gits mad at y'all, she'll put a hex on y'all."

When we pulled up, the old woman sed, "I wanna buy a small fish for 50 cents."

I sed, "Ok." And I give 'er the biggest one we had. She sed she jist wanted a small one, but I told 'er she could have any one she wanted.

She sed, "I'll jist take the one y'all give me." She give us 50 cents.

I looked at Sam and handed 'er the 50 cents and sed, "It's y'all's. Y'all sed we'd split it. So this time y'all keep it, and I'll keep it the next time."

She told me, "Thank y'all for the kiss." Be still, my heart.

I got Kate, and told Sam I'd take 'er home. My brother come down to the dock and I asked if'n he'd take my share of the fish home. I got on Kate, and Sam got on behind me and held 'er fish. I asked if'n she knowed how to clean them fish, and if'n she would show me how.

She sed, "Shore." So she cleaned 'em real slow. Now I know jist how to do it.

Her dad come out and thanked me for the fish and told me Sam could go fishin' 'bout any time. I got on Kate and were ready to leave when she sed, "Bye."

Her sister were watchin' at the door, but Sam looked at me and sed, "I'd kiss y'all but my sister will kid me 'bout it."

As I were in bed that night I thought 'bout that kiss. I shore liked it.

My brother done cleaned all 'em fish. My mama give some to the people who live down the road. They helped clean up the place afore. The place we live in now is bigger and closer to the water. But them snakes and skeeters is jist as bad.

I got up 'bout 6:00. My dad were gone. So I asked my mama where he were, and she sed he were gone to Sawtown to get a job.

I sed, "I thought we was gonna fish for a livin'."

She told me that he could make a better livin' sharpenin' saw blades, but he'd be home on Friday.

I got Kate out and went to git Sam to see if'n she knowed how to set the crab traps. Kate were real slow, and I were in a hurry to get there.

Sam were washin' dishes. I asked 'er if'n she knowed how to set the traps.

She sed, "I shore do."

James Carlton Fussell

Settin' Crab Traps

Chapter 11

I were settin' on the porch when Sam's little sister come up and set down by me. Then she sed, "Did y'all kiss my sister?" My face turned 'bout as red as a fox's behind in pokeberry season. I jist smiled at 'er.

Sam finished washin' the dishes, and we needed to get them fish guts put in them traps. I sed, "How many traps you got? I got 10 traps."

She didn't know how many she had. So we got the fish guts and I helped 'er git on Kate. I put the guts up front of me and I got on the mule. We started down the road, and she put 'er arms 'round me. Boy! It shore felt good.

We got to the boat and put the traps in the boat. We put the crab box in for the crabs we catched. We put guts in each one of them traps. Then we put the traps out. She sed, "We smell like fish guts!" We jist laughed.

We went back to the shore to wait for the crabs to crawl in the traps. She seen the seine and sed, "Let's pull that seine."

I didn't know what she were talkin' 'bout. We put it in the boat and headed down the river toward the Gulf. We put the seine across the river and tied it to a post. It had a rock on the other end. We stretched it good.

"Now we wait for the tide to change," sed Sam.

I sed, "What's a tide?

And she sed, "When the water comes in and goes out every day."

The Mullet Boys

Setting the seine.

We was sittin' there talkin' and she leaned over and kissed me for a long time. I thought my heart would jist explode! It shore made me feel good. She sed, "It's time to check the seine."

So we stopped where the rock were at. The water shore were goin' out of the river. She sed, "We got somethin' big."

We pulled and pulled. Then we pulled up a dead man that the crabs had already et on. The tide were takin' 'im out. I grabbed for 'im, but all I got were 'is shoe. I shore wish I'd got both shoes. The seine were full of fish, but the man were gone.

I told 'er, "I don't think we should tell nobody about 'im." She thought so too.

We had a boatload of fish. We put the seine in the boat and she sed we had to dry the seine out. She showed me how.

We stopped at the crab traps. They was full! We had a box of crab, too! I grabbed 'er and told 'er she were the best fisherman I ever seen and hugged 'er. She felt good.

My mama were at the dock. She seen all 'em fish and sed, "We gotta smoke all 'em fish."

James Carlton Fussell

Tha same ole woman come down and wanted to buy some. I jist give 'em to 'er. She tried to pay me, but I sed, "No, y'all can have it." She jist smiled.

Then I sed, "Y'all want some crab too?"

She sed, "Yes!"

So I put 'em in a sack for 'er and told 'er, "No, y'all can't pay for 'em neither."

School

Chapter 12

My mama sed, "Y'all know y'all can't go fishin' tomorrow. We're gonna do some schoolin'."

Sam looked at 'er and asked, "Would y'all teach me to read?"

My mama sed, "I'd be glad to."

I told my mama that Sam has two sisters at home, and she sed, "Bring 'em along."

Now, I didn't like school, but if'n Sam were gonna be there, I'd like it!"

I got Kate and picked up Sam and 'er sisters to take 'em to our house for school. Them kids was all ready. They never been to school. So I put all of 'em on the back of Kate. They was goin' to school!

First, mama taught 'em their ABC's and then their numbers. They was real quick to learn and in less'n a month they was doin' purty good!

My dad come home. He were makin' 12 dollars a week, which were good pay. He brought lumber home to build a big smoker. Now I could catch all the mullet to smoke that I wanted. We started sellin' fish. Lewis had 'is boat and I had mine with Sam. Sam helped clean fish too. We threw the guts out on the dock. Them crabs'll come in and eat 'em.

A Storm

Chapter 13

Rain clouds was buildin' in the west. Sam sed, "Looks like a bad storm comin." She were good on guessin' the weather. They all listened to 'er. We pulled the boat out of the water and turned it up-side-down. I took Sam home on Kate, and she kissed me! My heart jist run away.

I left and started back home. I were jist 'bout home when the bottom fell out of the sky. It were rainin' so hard! I took Kate to the barn and dried 'er off and wiped 'er down. Then I run to the house. I were soakin' wet, so I changed my wet clothes and put on some dry ones.

We was lookin' out the window, watchin' it rain, and I seen a man in a boat havin' trouble. He were tryin' to land the boat. It were one of them men that were shootin' at each other out in the Gulf.

I run to the dock to hold the rope so he could get out and I tied the boat to the dock. I told 'im to git to the house. We both run as fast as we could. I told 'im I'd build a fire to dry us off.

The fire shore felt good. When we dried out, my mama fixed us somethin' to eat. She cooked some fish, grits, cat-eye biskits with home made grape jelly and a hot cup of coffee. I drank it black.

He were dressed purty good. And he had good-lookin' shoes. He wanted to know how close we was to Tampa.

The Mullet Boys

Fish and grits.

Sed, "It be 'bout 60 miles."

Then he wanted to know if'n we had a car. I told 'im, "No."

Next he asked if'n we had a horse, and could he buy a horse from us. I sed, "No. But Mr. Atz might have one."

He wanted to know if'n I would go with 'im to see Mr. Atz. I sed, "In this rain?"

And he sed, "Yes."

My mamma looked at me funny, but I sed, "I guess so. It's 'bout half a mile up the road."

He wanted to leave now. We walked through the rain to Mr. Atz's house. I knocked on the door. He opened the door and sed, "What are y'all doin' out in this rain?"

I sed, "This man wants to buy a horse."

The man asked, "How much do you want for it?"

Mr. Atz thought a minute and then sed, "Okay. Saddle and horse, 100 dollars."

The man sed, "Here's 150 dollars, But I need it now."

Mr. Atz looked at me and I looked at 'im. He sed, "Let me get my coat and hat." We went to the barn and saddled the horse.

The man handed me somethin'. I knowed it were money, but didn't know how much.

I asked the man what he wanted me to do with 'is boat.

He sed, "Y'all can have it."

I looked at Mr. Atz and he looked back. We stood at the barn door and watched the man ride off in the rain. He sure were in a hurry.

I walked back home. It were a cold rain, and I were shakin' real good. But I walked down to look at the boat. I took the pump and pumped all the water out and put it under the shelter afore goin' to the house.

I got home. The fire were goin' in the fire place. It shore felt good. I got me a cup of strong coffee and stood by the fireplace till my clothes dried out.

Then I 'membered the money he give me. My eyeballs 'bout fell out. They were a 500 dollar bill! I sed, "Mama, Mama, Mama!"

She sed. "What?"

"Look what he give me!"

She sed, "What y'all gonna do with it?"

I sed, "Let's build a nice house with it. I can catch the stage when it stops rainin' and see if'n Lewis Jr. or somebody can build it."

Lewis Jr. stayed in Tampa a lot. Mama sed he were a courtin'. Guess he seen me with Sam, and he wanted a girl friend. He found a good job too.

LEWIS JR.'S SURPRISE

Chapter 14

I caught the stage at the graveyard and paid my 3 dollars. It shore were a rough ride. I knowed Kate and Pete was slow, but they wasn't rough like the stage. We rode all day. They changed horses 'bout every 5 miles. But they was real quick.

We looked over on the side of the road. They were a man layin' there. It were the man that bought the horse from Mr. Atz. The horse were dead, too. A man come over and told us somebody kilt 'em. I don't know why anybody would kill a good horse for no reason.

The stage started back up. It shore were dusty. They were a big ole woman sittin' in there, and she smelt bad. They was 5 us on that stage. Nobody sed much. When we got to Tampa, I asked where the fish camp were, and they sed that for a dollar the man with them horses would take me.

So I asked 'im, and he sed, "Shore."

As we was ridin' I sed, "They was a dead man on the side of the road back there. He dressed real good."

He sed, "Them bad people, they shoot and kill all the time. Most of 'em live on the bay."

We got to the fish camp. They had one of them cars. I shore did want one of 'em some day. I had enough money to buy one now, but we needed an ice machine too.

I didn't know jist how to find Lewis Jr., but I headed up to the bench out front of a building when a man unlatched the door.

It were Lewis Jr. He sed, "What're y'all doin' here?"

I sed, "We need an ice machine."

He sed, "Them thangs cost lots of money."

So I sed, "How much?"

He told me, "'Bout 300 dollars."

I wanted to know where to find one, but he sed, "I'll have to find out."

The rest of them people in there now woke up, and they 'membered me, but I didn't 'member them. Then I seen why Lewis Jr. were there. The purty girl we seen a long time ago were there. When we moved to Homosassa I were 10, and I'm 16 now. We come a long way in jist 6 years.

Lewis Jr. talked with the man that owned the fish camp and he sed, "Tampa Ice Company builds them ice machines."

He told Lewis Jr. to git the car and take me to Tampa Ice Company. Now I never rode in a car afore. He pushed them 2 levers up and turned on a switch and pulled on the crank. I thought it were gonna blow up. He got in the seat beside the left lever. We was goin' forward. He put one of the levers down and it got goin' fast. I never moved that fast in my life.

They was a bunch of cars on the street. Then I seen a funny-lookin' car

and sed, "What's that?"

He sed, "That's a streetcar." It shore made a lot of noise. And it run on a track. We got to Tampa Ice Company. Well, I didn't have no shoes on and seen Lewis Jr. didn't like that a bit, but shoes hurt my feet.

The man come out and sed, "What can I do for y'all?"

Lewis Jr. sed, "Tell 'im what y'all want."

I told 'im that I wanted an ice machine.

He sed, "Y'all know y'all have to have a hit and miss engine and some ammonia, don't y'all?"

I sed, "Okay."

He sed, "Where do y'all live?"

Sed, "In Homosassa."

He asked, "How big a one do y'all want?" I jist looked at Lewis Jr.

Lewis spoke up and sed, "They want one where y'all make ice to sell."

The man sed, "I think I know jist what y'all need. Do y'all have any money?"

I sed, "Yes, Sir."

He sed, "This thang costs lots of money, but y'all can make y'all's money back. Do y'all have land?"

I sed, "Yes, Sir."

He sed, "How much?"

I jist sed, "Lots of land." He jist smiled.

Then he sed, "If'n I set it up, it will cost y'all 300 dollars."

So I sed, "When can y'all set it up?" He told me they would bring it by boat, and did we have a boat dock.

I told 'im, "Shore do."

He told me we would need to build a place to put the ice machine in, 'cause it can't be outside.

He wanted money afore he started to make it.

I sed, "How much do y'all need to start?"

He sed, "100 dollars."

Lewis Jr. sed he had that much. I didn't tell 'im I had 300 dollars. So he paid it and I told 'im I'd pay 'im back when we made the money back.

The man sed the ice machine would be built in 'bout a month.

Then Lewis told me somethin' that made my mouth fall wide open. He sed, "I got married 2 weeks ago, but don't y'all tell Mama."

James Carlton Fussell

I told 'im I had to git back home. But first 'is father-in-law and Lewis Jr. took me to a fancy restaurant. That's a place to eat. When I seen the prices, I wanted to leave, but they sed, "We's gonna eat here."

When we got up to leave, they left money layin' on the table, so I picked it up and give it back to 'em outside the eatin' place. But they sed that were a tip. Whatever that is.

Lewis Jr. took me to the stage coach and I paid my 3 dollars to ride back to Homosassa. They were an ole woman there to ride, too, jist the 2 of us. I had my money in my underwear, so if'n somebody robbed us they wouldn't git it. We rode all night long. The stage stopped and I got out. I had 'bout 5 miles to walk, and the sun were jist comin' up.

I 'membered the time them robbers was gonna rob me along there, so I went through the woods. I looked down the road and seen 'em in the bushes. So I slipped on by. I seen 3 horses with the Diamond X brand on it. It were that bad bunch from Inverness. I shore wished I had my gun with me. I hid in them bushes, but they stayed there 'bout 2 hours.

Then a wagon come by and they stopped it. It were Mr. Atz. They was gonna rob 'im. They hit 'im up the side of 'is head. One of their horses over on the side. They were a big oak tree there, and I thought, *If'n I can git to that horse, they's probably a gun on it.* I slipped through the woods there, and shore 'nuff, there were a rifle on it.

So I eased up and took that gun jist as that man was gonna hit Mr. Atz again. I shot 'is hand and y'all could see the blood jist fly. Them other 2 run for cover and I shot one. He fell. I couldn't see the third one, but I knowed he were there.

I heard a shot, and then another shot. Mr. Atz sed, "I got 'em. Who's out there?"

I walked out of the woods and he sed, "Well, Red Fussell, I shore am glad to see y'all!"

We took that sorry bunch and put 'em in a gator hole. They would make good gator food. We took them saddles and guns and kept 'em. I told Mr. Atz if'n we put a pine cone under them horse's tails, they'd run till they fall out.

He sed, "Let's do it."

So I found pine cones and put 'em under them horses' tails. I whacked them on the back side and they took off runnin'. We stood and watched 'em horses run wide open.

They was blood in the road so we kicked sand on it. I got on Mr. Atz's wagon to ride home with 'im. I told 'im 'bout the man he sold that horse to, that he were dead on the road. Somebody done kilt 'im.

He told me somebody got 'is boat too.

I told Mr. Atz that the man in Tampa sed they was a bad bunch.

I rode home with 'im and he took me to my house. I shore were glad to git home and git cleaned up. I went to sleep and when I woke up, the sun were shinin'.

I thought, *I think I'll go see Sam.* So I took Pete and rode up there to 'er house. I knocked on the door, but didn't get no answer. I looked inside. They was gone!

I didn't know what to do, so I rode back to the fish house. I asked Mama where they went.

She sed, "I seen 'em goin' with all their stuff, but I don't know where they was goin'."

I looked everywhere, but couldn't find 'em. They musta moved a long way off.

The Diamond X Chase

Chapter 15

I had to go to work to git ready for an ice house, 'cause they was comin' soon with our ice machine. I had to clear a spot out.

Afore long, I looked down river and here come our ice house. Them fellers unloaded it on the dock. They shore were a bunch of stuff. Mama fixed 'em a good lunch with some hot coffee.

They sed, "We'll start in the mornin'."

I shore wish I knowed where Sam was. I wanted to tell Mama that Lewis had a wife, but I didn't, 'cause Lewis Jr. told me not to.

They started makin' the buildin' to put the ice plant in. I were jist lookin' on.

It were Friday, but my dad hadn't come home yet. He jist took Kate with 'im.

I looked up and there he were comin', but he were layin' on the seat of the wagon. I run down to see what were wrong. He were dead. He'd been shot.

I seen Mama run to 'im. I looked on the seat and he done took 'is finger and made a diamond, then an X with 'is own blood. I knowed what he meant. I run to the house to git my gun, but my mama stopped me. "We gotta bury 'im," she sed.

Most everybody come 'round. Lewis Jr. come home and he helped me build a box to put 'im in. When the box were done, they put 'im in it. The next day they put 'im in the ground. I shore am gonna miss 'im.

The man from Sawtown sed them killers done kilt 3 men and stole all their money. The big boss sed he would give 50 dollars to anyone who finds out who kilt 'em.

It rained that afternoon. Mr. Atz come by and I told 'im I were gonna git that bunch from the Diamond X. I showed 'im what Dad put on the seat afore he died.

He sed, "Come by and git a good horse."

I sed, "I'll pay y'all for it."

I give my mama the money for the ice house. She begged me, "Don't go git 'em big men. Y'all don't even weigh 100 pounds."

I sed, "I know, but I gotta go."

So she give me 20 dollars back so I could have somethin' to eat. I got my small rifle, 2 boxes of bullets and a bunch of smoked mullet. I put 'em all in the bag on the side of the horse. Mr. Atz sed this were a real quiet horse, to just rub 'is neck and he wouldn't say nothin'.

When I got on the horse my mama sed, "I done lost y'all's dad; I don't wanna lose y'all, too."

I sed, "I gotta go." Jist 'bout everybody round here watched me go. I thought, I shore hope I do come back.

Lewis told Mama if'n she needed 'im to come home, to give the stage coach driver a note and 50 cents; he had to git back to Tampa to run the fish camp.

I rode through the night to Dade City and camped in the woods. Fed the horse. Give 'im some water and rubbed 'im down.

The Tampa paper got wind of me leavin' to go find the killers that kilt my dad. I shore wish they hadn'ta did that.

The smoked mullet shore were good. I miss Sam. I didn't even know 'er real name, but I were shore in love with 'er. The night were cold, but I knowed I couldn't build no fire. This were a fight for my life.

The next day I eased 'round town lookin' in a beer joint or wherever I thought they might be. I done that for 'bout a week, but no luck. I were 'bout ready to give up when I seen a Dimond X brand on a horse. I hid when he got on 'is horse and I got on mine. I stayed in the woods, and then turned to go through the swamp. I took my spy glass out that I got out of a boat. It were a moonlight night so I could see through it. They were an ole shack next to the woods. They's where he went.

James Carlton Fussell

So I eased on through the woods. I could see a dim light in the house. Ever once in a while I seen somebody. I backed off to let things settle down. I didn't need to rush nothin'. When daylight broke, he come out on the porch. I'd made me a piece for the end of my rifle so nobody couldn't hear it fire. I were gettin' ready to fire, and here come a rider. He were ridin' fast like someone were chasin' 'im.

So I quickly shot the one on the porch. He had stopped rockin'. I fired and he fell to the floor. I'd put the bullet right in 'is ear, so you can't tell why he died. The rider kept comin'. He walked up on the porch and looked my way then turned. I fired. He fell too. I hadn't seen the third one, but he run. I couldn't shoot 'im 'cause he went through the swamp. I better not go after 'im.

I walked up to the house to see 'em. I wanted to shoot 'em again, but I didn't. I knowed that one that run would soon be after me. Their horses was here. If'n I took 'em with me they would hang me for horse thief. So I took 'em to where my horse were, and looked in the side of the bag on the horses. They were my dad's pay slip with 'is name on it, but the 12 dollars weren't there. I thought, *Got 2 of them, Dad.* Now I needed to put a pine cone under them horse tails and watch 'em run.

News traveled fast and everybody knowed that a red-headed boy done shot 2 of 'em. I wish they hadn'ta did that. They was 4 of 'em that did the robbin'.

That night it were cold and rainin'. It were a bad night and I were camped under an ole oak. I heard a voice, "Hey, Red. I ain't got no gun. Come with me and get out of this cold." I didn't know if'n I should, but guessed if'n he wanted to shoot me he woulda did it already.

So I git my horse and walked behind 'im. I put my horse in the barn, fed 'im some of that man's corn and we both went inside. They was 'is wife and 2 small girls.

"This here's Red Fussell. He's chasin' them killers."

His wife looked at me and sed, "Y'all don't weigh 100 pounds soakin' wet."

I sed, "I'm small; but I have a brother, and he's real big."

The fire shore felt good. Sed, "I still got 2 men to find. I shore am glad you invited me in.

Then she sed, "They kilt my boy the same day they kilt your dad." I looked at 'er and they was tears in 'er eyes.

I told 'em both, "I will hunt 'em till I git them all."

The man sed, "Want me to go with y'all?"

But I sed, "No, I may not come back. Y'all need to stay here and take care of them girls."

The man sed, "One of them men is real bad."

I asked if'n he knowed where he hung out, and did he have a Diamond X on 'is horse.

He sed, "Yes. He does."

I asked, "Do you know where he lives?"

He sed, "'Bout 3 miles down the road. He don't work; he jist steals."

I asked 'im how many men lived in that house.

He sed, "Well it's not really a house, more like a shack; but he's not always there."

I told 'em I'd be leavin' in the mornin' and laid down, but couldn't go to sleep. I heard somethin' outside and looked out the window. I seen the man of the house slip out, git 'is horse, and ride off to the left. I began to wonder if'n he were one of them killers, so I git up and git my horse.

I followed 'is tracks to an ole house. I got my spy glass out, and seen a man through the window. That's the man I were lookin' for. So I set there and watched for 'im to come outside. The man with them little girls left after a few minutes and rode back toward 'is house. When daylight broke, out stepped the man that had run from the ole shack afore; he were the one I were lookin' for. I put a bullet in 'is ear and he fell. Then another man stepped out of the house to see what were goin' on, and I put a bullet in 'is ear, too.

I looked in the men's bags on the side of their horses. They were 12 dollars that were my dad's. That were 'is salary for the whole week. I took it, took the saddles off, put a pine cone under the horse's tails and they run.

I thought, *Should I go back where that man was gonna git me kilt? No, I need to go.*

I got on my horse. I had 2 good days to ride to git back home. I stopped at a store to git me one of them soda waters and somethin' to eat.

I put 'em on the counter and asked the man, "How much?"

The man recognized me as the red-headed boy who kilt them men and sed, "Them's mean, boy. Robbed me once, hit me with a gun. They was 3 of 'em. Then a runt like y'all fought 'em all! If'n they's anythin' else y'all want here, y'all jist take it."

I sed, "I can pay for it."

He sed, "No." And 'is wife come out and give me a hug around my neck. I shore miss Sam. 'Afore I left, a bunch of people shook my hand. They was all scared of 'em. But so were I. I fed my horse with some corn the man give me and left.

I were tired, so I stopped at a house and asked if'n I could sleep in their barn. The man sed, "Shore can."

His son told 'is dad who I were, and the son sed, "Y'all can have my bed." But I told 'im the barn would do jist fine.

They fixed supper. It were real good. I told 'em if'n they ever was in Homossasa, to stop and I'd give 'em a meal.

Their young boy sed, "Was y'all scared?"

I sed, "I shore was."

He sed, "Did y'all sleep on the ground in the rain?"

I sed, "I shore did."

He asked if'n it were fun, but I told 'im it warn't and I hoped he never had to do it.

The man looked at me and I could tell somethin' were botherin' 'im. He sed, "They kilt my boy. I shoulda kilt 'em all, but I were 'fraid of 'em. I jist want to thank y'all."

I crawled in the hay and laid there. I heard someone come in. It were 'is wife. She done brought me a blanket. Then she sed, "He really misses that boy. Would y'all stay here?"

I told 'er I couldn't, that I needed to go and help my mama.

I got up the next mornin' and saddled up the horse. The lady come out and told me to eat afore I left. They done made a big breakfast of everythin' I like. When I went to leave, I took that 12 dollars and put it under the plate and left. I 'membered what Ray sed, "Don't never be greedy."

(My dad were kilt on the west side of the Lachoochee Forest. I kilt them men that shot Dad at Trilby, near Floral City.)

Back Home

Chapter 16

I rode all day and seen the road to turn in to our house, but thought maybe that crook were near, so I went through the woods. I jist got down the road when I turned. They's a bunch of people cheerin' and wavin'. I thought, What for? It were for me, but I didn't need it.

When I got home I took me a hot bath. I hadn't had one for 36 days, so I knowed I smelt bad. I shaved for the first time in a while and put on clean clothes. That shore felt good. I walked down to look at the ice house.

Nobody wanted the boy that took care of the ice house to be 'round my mama. Guess they didn't trust 'im.

But Mama sed, "He's in charge of the ice house and he lives in the back there." We went back up to the house, and she told me he done a real good job.

I asked her if'n she heard from Sam, but she sed, "No."

In 'bout a week the man come from Sawtown. He wanted me to go to Inverness with 'im. He had one of 'em Model T's. I shore want one of 'em some day. I sed, "Shore."

When we started to leave he sed, "Wanna drive?"

I sed, "I don't know how."

He sed, "I'll teach y'all when we git on the open road."

After a little while I caught on jist how to do it. I asked what we was goin' to Inverness for, but he sed, "Jist to be goin'."

I shore did like drivin' faster in the car than ridin' a horse. We got to Inverness in 'bout 2 hours. That were real quick. Even with a good horse it would be all day. He told me to turn, and then to stop. We was at the Ford place. They had all kinds of 'em Model T's. I liked the one with the rumble seat.

We got out and went inside. They were my mama. How'd she git there?

They were a blanket under the Model T with somethin' under it. The man from the Sawtown, where Dad worked, sed, "The Model T's y'all's, but y'all have to take what's under it."

I sed, "What's under it?"

He jist sed, "Go look."

They warn't a sound. It were all quiet. I raised the blanket, and there were Sam!!! She kissed me in the mouth, right in front of everyone!

I told 'em, "Y'all can keep the Model T, but I git Sam."

I ain't never been so happy. They hollered and clapped their hands. And there stood my brother, too. I ain't seen 'im in a long time. I were really glad to see 'im. He sed, "I shore worried 'bout y'all. I'm glad it worked out this way, and y'all got the girl."

The man from Sawtown got up and made a speech 'bout what I done. Some of it were bad, but it hada be did. Then Lewis took Mama home. He went back to Tampa. I were there with Sam, and I sed, "Let's git married."

She sed, "Y'all will have to ask my dad first." I were scared to ask 'im, but when we got to Homosassa, I went in the house to see 'er dad.

I sed, "I-I-I."

Sam's dad finally sed, "Spit it out, boy."

My heart were a-beatin' so fast and my mouth were dry.

Then Sam's mama jist sed, "Yes."

I were so happy then.

Her dad sed, "We'll have red-headed little ones 'round here."

My mama bought Sam a weddin' dress. My brother had a church buildin' built in Homosassa. Since he had been workin' in Tampa, he had lots of money and he paid for everythin'.

My Weddin'

Chapter 17

We was married in Homossasa in the new Homosassa Church. Sam's sisters was the flower girls, and Lewis Jr. stood up with me. My mama made us a cake, and all the neighbors come to see us wed.

We went for a boat ride to Cuba with a load of cows and stayed there for several months. It shore were fun!! When we got back to Homosassa, my brother done built us a house. I thanked 'im. It were real nice.

We moved our stuff into the new house. When I seen the shoe I picked up in that boat, I started to throw it out. But Sam seen somethin' in it. She pulled a paper out of the shoe and unfolded it. It were a map.

I sed, "That's Shell Island."

She sed, "It shore is."

I sed, "Tomorrow we'll go there. You know, I bet that were what all 'em people was fightin' about in 'em boats. They don't come 'round no more."

So the next day we got a shovel and we headed to Shell Island. Sam sed, "Don't stop here. Go on down and pull up over there."

I didn't know what she were doin', but I stopped. She jist kissed me like I never been kissed afore. Then she sed, "I'm gonna have a baby!"

Whoee! Were I happy! But I'll have to work even harder.

We come to Shell Island and seen a stump on the map. It showed a tree and it sed to dig in the middle of the stump. So we looked 'round till we found what we thought were the right stump, and I started diggin'. Nothin' there.

But Sam sed, "Dig deeper." So I put the shovel in and dug some more. I hit somethin' hard. We dug 'round it. It were a big ole metal box, but we couldn't lift it up. So I thought, *If'n I could just break the lock with somethin' heavy.*

I went back to the boat to find somethin' that'd work, and brought back the anchor. I swung that thang hard, and the lock done broke!!! We raised the lid, but neither of us sed nothin'. We jist looked with our mouths hangin' wide open. It were full of gold!!!

I picked up one piece and handed it to Sam. She still hadn't sed nothin'. So we carried the gold pieces to the boat, and then lifted the metal box up and took it to the boat. We put the gold back in the metal box and run the boat back home. We got some bags and carried the gold up to our house. Then put it back in the metal box. I sed, "Tomorrow we're gonna count it and give y'all's dad a quarter of it and Lewis Jr. a quarter of it.

So the next day we loaded up Sam's dad's quarter share and took the car to 'is house. When we walked in the door 'er mama were cryin'. She sed, "We all gonna lose our house. We can't pay back what we borrowed."

But I sed, "Shore y'all can!" And I showed 'em the gold.

Sam's dad sed, "No, y'all need it."

But I told 'im that we didn't need it. And I sed, "Let's go to the bank and pay it off right now."

So we went to the bank and give 'im a gold piece, and he give us the change back. Then he looked at me real hard and sed, "Y'all are Red Fussell, ain't y'all?"

I sed, "I shore is." He handed the money back and sed, "Y'all saved me a bunch of money when y'all got rid of 'em bad boys."

I sed, "I can pay it. It is now paid." We went back to the house.

I could tell somethin' else were still botherin' Sam's dad, so then he told us Sam's younger sister, Sally, up in Inverness, well, 'er husband beats 'er all the time when he gits drunk.

I sed, "Let's go see 'er." We knocked on the door and she come to the door. Her eye were all black. He done got drunk again and beat 'er.

So I asked where he were at, and she sed, "At the beer joint."

The Mullet Boys

I took the car to the beer joint. When I walked in he seen me and sed, "Well, if'n it ain't Red Fussell!"

I sed, "It shore are. Y'all's beatin' y'all's wife and I don't like it. Anybody can whip a runt like y'all. Shore can. Which one of y'all boys would like to make 10 dollars?"

One guy sed, "What I got to do?"

I sed, "Make both 'is eyes black."

He sed, "Then y'all will pay me 10 dollars?"

I sed, "Yes."

So he knocked 'im half way across the room. His nose were bleedin' real good.

I sed, "Now y'all know how it feels!" And I handed the man 'is 10 dollars. I sed, "Any time he hits a woman, black 'is eye again and I'll give y'all 'nother 10 dollars."

Them other boys sed, "Well, what 'bout us?"

Sed, "The same goes for y'all."

I went back to Sally's house and told 'er to pack 'er clothes. She were goin' with us. She give me a hard time 'bout it, but I jist told 'er to go pack. We all left Inverness and headed home. I told my mama to teach Sally how to run the store, so Mama didn't have to work so hard. My mama done took the ice house and made it into a store, so I knowed she could use some help.

Off to Bank in Tampa

Chapter 18

I asked Sam if'n she wanted to go with me to Tampa, but she sed she didn't feel so good. So I filled the tank full of gas and checked the oil. I put the gold under the seat. It looked like rain, but the car had a top, so I weren't worried 'bout no rain. I left in the mornin' and had my pistol and shotgun next to me, jist in case.

I'd been gone 'bout 20 miles when I seen a rider in them woods. That's what 'em crooks do. When I went by, he shot in front of me. I thought shore I were gonna be robbed. I stopped, and he were right on me. He looked at me and sed, "Sorry, Mr. Red. I'll rob somebody else."

I sed, "Why are y'all robbin' people?"

And he sed, "My wife's real sick, and the doctor sed he wouldn't see 'er if'n I ain't got no money, or a hog, or a chicken to give 'im."

I sed, "Well, how much do y'all need?"

He sed, "5 dollars."

I asked 'im why he didn't get a job, and he sed he couldn't find one.

So I sed, "I'll give y'all 5 dollars to go to Homassasa, and y'all tell my mama I sed to give y'all a job."

I started my Model T again. It shore do run good. I made it to Tampa in real good time. Lewis Jr. gassed up a big boat and the man paid 'im. He waved from the boat and left. I asked 'im, "How's business?"

He sed, "It's slow, but I ain't worried."

The Mullet Boys

I sed, 'Yes, y'all is. I can tell. Do you 'member that shoe I grabbed off that dead man when Sam and I was seinin' for fish. 'Member, when all the fightin' were goin' on?"

He sed, "Shore, I 'member."

I told 'im 'bout the map in the shoe, and told 'im, "Here's y'all's part of the gold." I told 'im that Mama now had help for the store and purty soon she could quit. Sam and me had enough to keep us goin', and that we was fixin' to have a baby. By now Lewis Jr. had three little girls. So I asked 'im how they was. He told me that they was doin' good.

But he sed, "Afore y'all leave, I got someone for y'all to see." He sed, "You know 'im?"

I sed, "No I don't think so."

He sed, "Do you 'member when we was movin' to Homosassa? We stopped by the family with the big fire and we et with 'em."

"Shore, I remember 'em. Glad to see y'all. Your family doin' all right?"

He told me they was.

So I handed Lewis Jr. 'is gold, and told 'im to do whatever he wanted with it, but I needed to get back home. I had thangs to do. I always 'membered what Ray sed, "Never be greedy." We'd been blessed.

I left Tampa and stopped at a gas station to fill the car with gas and check the oil. As I started out an ole man sed, "How far y'all goin'?"

I sed, "'Bout 60 miles."

He wanted to ride with me. As we traveled he told me 'bout 'is wife and how 4 of 'is boys become crooks. They killed and robbed people, and one day people got enough of it and kilt 'em all.

So everybody hates 'im, and 'is wife died with a broken heart. Sed, "I jist wander from place to place. Nobody cares if'n I live or die."

We traveled 'bout 30 miles and he sed, "Let me off where that light's at."

I give 'im all the change I had to get 'im somethin' to eat. He thanked me and walked off in the dark. I knowed who he were. I done kilt all 'is boys. They was the bunch that kilt my own dad. I felt sad for 'im. He has no one. I wanted to help 'im, but I jist couldn't do it.

I got home and shore were glad to be there. I checked with one fisherman that worked for us at the store. He sed the store were doin' fine. Sally were learnin' how to run the store real fast. Sam were gettin' big as a barn. The ice man were as happy as could be, and everybody laughed

James Carlton Fussell

at 'im. He were purty funny, but he worked hard, too. Seemed like everybody were happy and thangs was goin' good, except Sam were sick every mornin'.

I got news one day that Sally's husband were kilt in a bar fight. I didn't know if'n I should tell Sally or not, but Sam told me I should. So I went to the store, and got me a cup of coffee. Then I told 'er he'd been kilt in a bar fight. I seen a tear come in 'er eye and she sed, 'He weren't bad till he drank, but I loved 'im."

One of Sam's sisters, Judy, moved to Okahumpka. Her and 'er husband had a big orange grove. They had 5 kids. Guess they didn't know what caused 'em.

L'il Bill

Chapter 19

Sam had a baby boy. Mr. Atz come down every day jist so he could hold 'im. Mr. Atz's name were Bill, so we named our baby, Bill. That man were jist so happy 'bout that. He called our baby his baby, and Alice, 'is wife would say he were jist a crazy ole man. And then she jist laughed. We let 'em take Bill home with 'em sometimes, and they spoiled 'im rotten. Guess we need to have 'nother baby.

My mama weren't doin' so good, so we took 'er to the doctor in Inverness. But the doctor sed he couldn't do nothin' for 'er. Two weeks later she died in 'er sleep. I give the stage coach driver 50 cents with a note to Lewis sayin', "Mama died". The next day he were here with 'is family. He's got 3 good-lookin' girls. I had a casket made; she already had a head stone I made for 'er when I made Dad's. It were already right next to Dad's grave. We put 'er in the ground. I thanked everybody 'round here for comin'. It shore were a long day.

A man come up to me and sed, "Do y'all know me?" I didn't recognize 'im.

He sed, "I'm the man that tried to git y'all kilt." I jist looked at 'im.

He sed, "I hope y'all can forgive me. When y'all was chasin' 'em killers, I told 'em where y'all was at, but y'all left 'afore they could git there. I've woke up many a night thinkin' y'all would come back and kill me. My wife done left me when she found out what I'd done. I done it for the money, but now I done lost everythin."

I sed, "I thought 'bout killin' y'all, but jist let it go. I have no reason to kill y'all." But I felt sorry for 'im, 'cause we gotta live with what we done.

I asked Lewis and 'is family to eat with us. Sam's sister, Sally, done fixed a big meal, and people brought all kinds of food over. We talked 'bout old times. He talked 'bout leavin' Tampa, but 'is wife liked it there. I told 'im I would never leave Homosassa; I liked it here.

As time went on, Bill were gettin' bigger, and we had 'nother baby boy. We named 'im John. Bill were as bad as me when I were little, and John were a runt like me.

Lewis sed, "People in Tampa still 'member what y'all done to 'em killers. Sometimes they ask how big y'all was. Told 'em y'all didn't weigh more'n 100 pounds. And they'd jist look at me."

We heard the shrimp boat start up, but no one were shrimpin' today. We looked out there. It backed up with the tide and there were little Bill. I told 'im to turn off that motor. I tore up 'is butt.

Bill sed, "But I were jist goin' for a ride." He were only 5 years old!!!

Lewis laughed and sed, "Y'all shore got y'all's hands full!"

I sed, "Yes, we do. He's always into somethin'. Wonder what it will be like when he's 16?"

Lewis sed they had to be gettin' back. Sed, "Gotta go sell gas and bait. We sell a lot of it, and we're makin' good money. Shore wish Dad coulda had some of it. He worked so hard for what little he got. I guess we live as good as anyone, but we've had our ups and downs."

Visitin' Okahumpka

Chapter 20

We could see Mr. Atz were comin' up the road, and Lewis Jr. sed he hada git on 'is way. So he sed, "I gotta go. I'll see y'all."

Mr. Atz come and set on the porch and sed, "Tell y'all what y'all should do. Y'all should take Sam and git away for a few days. We'll look after the kids. We had 2 boys, too."

I sed, "I think y'all's right."

I told Sam, "Let's go to y'all's sister Judy's house in Okahumpka for a few days." So I gassed up the Model T and checked the oil and the tires. I didn't have to do that with Pete and Kate. Saturday we left. The road were better now and we could go much faster, but not too fast. The weather looked real good.

We went through Inverness and through some small towns, through Panasoffkee and on to Center Hill. They was lots of people there now. We stopped at Dr. Cherry's Drug Store to git us an ice cream. I told Sam we should sell ice cream in the store, but she sed she'd eat it all; and we both laughed.

We left Center Hill and on to Okahumpka, jist 9 miles down the road. She looked at me and sed, "Do y'all wanna move back?"

I sed, "No, I never could move. We done everythin' together in Homosassa."

James Carlton Fussell

Jack and Judy lived on Clear Water Lake. It were a real nice place. We pulled up in the driveway, and Sam's sister come out jist a hollerin'!! She were so glad to see Sam. Them 5 kids of 'ers had shore growed up. They all worked; they all went to school in Okahumpka. It's a big school, a good school. They bought more land, and they had about 100 acres for cows.

They was havin' trouble with cow thieves. I sed, "Jist shoot 'em."

Judy sed, "I would if'n I knowed who it is." She sed, "The sheriff's lookin' in to it."

I laughed and sed, "It might be 'im."

Her husband sed, "I shore hope not." He saddled up two horses, and we rode out on 'is land. It were fenced. I didn't like the fence, but it's not mine. Somethin' caught my eye and I sed, "Did y'all see that?"

He sed, "No."

I got off my horse and looked at the ground for tracks. There it were. "I know what's killin' y'all's cows."

He sed, "What's that?"

Sed, "It's a big cat. I seen it when it jumped. They's the track. Do y'all know anybody with dogs?"

Jack sed, "Shore do. Ray down the road has dogs."

I sed, "We can take the dogs and run it to the swamp. The cat'll run up a tree, and the dogs'll keep it up there till we can kill it."

That night we went to 'is friend Ray's house. So I thought when we got there to ask 'bout 'em dogs. He sed he didn't own 'em dogs. They belonged to 'is wife, Jane. So we asked Jane if'n we could borrow 'em dogs.

She sed, "No, but if'n I can go on the hunt, y'all can use 'em. What y'all gonna hunt?"

I sed, "A big ole cat!"

She sed she seen a big cat on the south side of 'em ditches in the big pasture. So she sed, "Tomorrow night we'll go cat huntin'."

We went home on Clear Water Lake and set down to rest afore we et supper. If'n I had 5 kids like them, I think I'd jist leave home. The oldest boy asked me, when I was chasin' them killers, did I think they might kill me.

I told 'im, "Yes, I were scared 'cause I thought they jist might."

The next day we looked at Jack's orange groves, and et a green orange. It warn't bad. The young boys of 'is drove the truck, and at the end of the day we et supper early and left to go to Ray and Jane's. I never knowed their last names.

We got to Ray and Jane's. They had the dogs all ready to go. We was on horseback. Ray had a good-lookin' horse and Jane rode a mule. It looked okay. She wore an ole pair of pants, and had 'er cow horn to blow so she could get 'er dogs back home. They's 'bout 12 of 'em. They's good-lookin' dogs.

When we started out, she asked if'n anybody got a chew. I wanted to laugh, but Sam's brother-in-law give 'er one. He knowed she chewed. We started down by the railroad track. The dogs didn't make no noise. We headed to 'is pasture and that ole blue dog opened up. We got a race on. It headed to the swamp, then it turned to Reed Hammock, then turned again. Them dogs was hot on that cat's tail. Then they was comin' back by us. The closer 'em dogs come, the faster Jane chewed. It were funny to watch.

Them dogs was on a real track. They turned again and went through their yard, and Jane sed, "I seen it! Shore are a big cat!!" We already knowed it were a big cat. It went to the west side of Clear Water Lake then turned east. That went right through 'is pasture. We heard the dogs bay.

Jane had a light on 'er head and she shined it up the tree. There it were! Sam's brother-in-law raised 'is gun to shoot it, but then brought 'is gun back down and sed, "I need to let 'im live." I jist smiled. I liked that.

They caught the dogs, put 'em on a rope so they wouldn't run off, and then we went back to Ray and Jane's. She sed, "I'll make a pot of coffee." I thought, *I'll bet 'er house is real dirty*, but when she opened the door, it were real clean. She spit out 'er chew and washed out 'er mouth, fed 'er dogs, and then we had a real good cup of coffee.

We drank our coffee, and she sed, "That cat always runs the same way every year. I'm shore glad y'all didn't shoot 'im. He'll be gone for a while, but he comes through here 'bout once a year. If'n y'all want, I'll pay for them cows. I love that cat."

As we set there I heard that cat scream. It raised the hair on my head. But she sed, "He always does that. He's been doin' that for years. I jist love it."

We went back to Clear Water Lake and et some sour orange pie. It shore were good. The next mornin' we et breakfast, and Sam sed, "We best be goin' home." Sam told Judy that we had give the store to Sally after Red's mama died, and she were doin' real good. We shook hands, hugged, sed our good-byes, and drove off.

Sour orange pie
3 larg sour oranges
foor Eggs seperated
14 oz sweetened milk
1 C. whipping Cream
Graham cracker crust

Heat oven to 350 degrees
Grate about half of the orange
Juice the oranges (no seeds)
2/3 c Juice
Beat Egg yolks grated Juice And milk
pour in crust
Bake 15-20 minutes on it Thickened
Cool
whip cream for pie

I sed, "Let's go by Sawtown. It'll be a little out of the way, but not much. So we went through Green Swamp. It were a little muddy, but we made it. Then we drove to Sawtown and stopped at the sawmill's main office. When I walked in, the man seen me and sed, "Hey, Red! What brings y'all this way?"

Sed, "We jist passin' through."

He asked, "Did y'all ever see this here picture of y'all and Sam?" We was shore young then. I went outside to get Sam to see the picture. She laughed.

We told 'im we had to go, but he wanted us to meet somebody. So I sed, "Okay." Out walked an ole man.

He sed, "Y'all's dad shore were a good worker. Shore hated when they kilt 'im. If'n it weren't for y'all, there probably woulda been a lot more kilt. I always thought y'all was a big man like y'all's dad, but, nope, y'all's jist a little runt. All the people 'round here don't think so. They'd do anythin' for y'all."

I told 'em, "We gotta go now. But thank y'all again for the car. I shore do like it... and HER!" Sam jist laughed.

As we was leavin', Sam asked me, "Would y'all take the car or me now?"

Sed, "That ain't a fair question", and we both laughed. When we turned on the road to Homosassa it were almost dark. I shore were glad to be back home. We didn't stop by Mr. Atz's house to pick up the kids. We jist went home, put on our night clothes and I held Sam in my arms and sed, "I love y'all, Sam."

The next mornin' we got ready to git the kids. I knocked on the door. Them kids come a-runnin' and grabbed me. I sed, 'It's time to go home."

But little Bill sed, "I am home." I jist laughed.

I looked at Mrs. Atz and she had tears in 'er eyes. "Y'all don't know what them kids mean to us. We couldn't love 'em any more if'n they was ours."

I sed, "They are y'all's, but they's gonna go with us now."

I looked at Bill and pointed to the door.

He sed, "Okay." He looked 'round and sed, "I'll see y'all, Grandma Alice." I seen 'er heart jist light up. We couldna ask for no better friends.

Fishin'

Chapter 21

We got 3 shrimp boats and 2 small boats to pull seines. We was learnin' that with the shrimp boats, they go all the way 'round the state of Florida, maybe to Texas, if'n the shrimpin' were good. The boat captain got paid by how many shrimp they caught, and the mullet boats got paid by the pound.

The shrimp made more money, and young boys pulled the seines. On a good day, they could make 200 dollars a day. They caught them catfish, too. All them catfish was good for was chum, and it only made 'bout 25 dollars a day, so they didn't do that if'n it could be helped.

At night, they had to fix the seines if'n they got a hole in it. We'd ice the fish down and ship 'em by train everywhere. And I shipped frogs and turtles, and some gator, but not much.

I were settin' on the dock one day and up come a man. He sed, "I'm lookin' for Red Fussell."

I sed, "What do y'all want to see 'im 'bout?"

He sed, "I'll tell 'im."

Well, it didn't strike me right, so I sed, "He left yesterday and won't be back for a week."

Mr. Atz were sittin' there with me and he done laughed.

The man sed, "He'll see me, or he'll be sorry."

I sed, "Sorry for what?"

The Mullet Boys

Shrimp Boat
by Sandy Oard Kruse

I could tell he were gittin' hot under the collar. I finally sed, "Look, if'n y'all wanna see me, jist say so. I'm Red Fussell."

He sed, "Well, y'all ain't as big as a rabbit."

I sed, "I didn't grow much." He went on to tell me that he were from New York City and wanted to write a story 'bout me killin' the crooks.

I sed, "No thank y'all. I done somethin' I ain't proud of, and I just wanna let it go."

He sed, "They's good money in it."

But I told 'im, "I don't need no money."

The man really wanted to do it and sed, "This here's y'all's last chance."

I sed, "Good."

He sed, "Who's the man settin' next to y'all?" I told 'im that were my friend, Mr. Atz, and that he were the best friend I got.

Sam called to me and I went to the house. She sed, "Set down. I got somethin' I need to tell y'all." It scared me. I thought somethin' awful happened. She sed, "We gonna have another baby, and I shore hope it's a girl, and I wanna name 'er Alice." This weren't bad news. I wondered what the boys'd think. They probably won't care.

So Friday I took 'er to the doctor in Inverness, and he sed she shore were gonna have a baby. Sam's sister, Sally, were happy 'bout it, too.

Sally were gettin' married the next month to a farmer livin' 'bout 3 miles from here. I shore hope she don't close the store, but she owns it, so guess she can do whatever she wants to.

A few days later, Sam called to me. She sounded frantic. Bill were gone, so she went down to Mrs. Atz to look. He weren't there. We looked and called, but we couldn't find 'im. We looked everywhere, and I were gettin' scared, too. Then I heard one of 'em boys out on the mullet boat holler. Bill were asleep on the boat. Guess workin' on the fishin' boat made 'im tired.

Sam wanted to wake 'im to come home, but I told 'er I'd jist carry 'im. When we got 'im back home he smelt like a mullet. And when 'is mama got through with 'is behind, he thought he were a mullet. He told me he were gonna go live with Grandma Alice.

I sed, "Well, y'all better go ask y'all's mama afore y'all go." He jist looked at me. I thought it were funny.

New Baby

Chapter 22

Our baby were born. But that little girl turned out to be another boy. The doctor told us we shouldn't have no more babies, so he fixed Sam so she couldn't. Sam's heart were jist no good no more.

Well, not havin' no more babies were fine by me. We named our new baby boy Richard, but he weren't a very strong baby, and we lost 'im 3 days later. That were real hard to go through. It 'bout broke Sam's heart. We buried 'im next to Mama and Dad.

I were settin' on the dock with Mr. Atz. My boys was givin' the ice man a real hard time. They'd ring the bell and run. He'd come out front, and there'd be nobody there.

We looked down the road and here come 2 riders They come to the dock. The horses they was ridin' was the best lookin' horses I ever seen. The saddles was silver inlaid. I knowed they was somebody important. He had 'em shiny boots, one of 'em fancy shirts, two pearl-handled pistols, a badge, and a big Stetson hat.

He sed, "This here's my wife." She were beautiful, and she were dressed jist like 'im. She had two pearl-handled pistols like 'is. In the scabbard she had a rifle. It were a Henry rifle, one of them new guns. Her boots shined like 'is, and she had on a badge. She shore were dressed nice with a Stetson hat, too. She looked good.

James Carlton Fussell

The man sed, "Do y'all know Henry Wall?"

I sed, "What do y'all want 'im for?"

He sed, "Ain't none of y'all's business."

So I sed, "I don't know 'im."

He looked at me real hard and sed, "If'n y'all know 'im and don't tell me, I'll put y'all in jail."

His wife sed, "Let's start over again. This here's my husband. We work together. We's G-men. We's chasin' crooks. We's not after Mr. Wall; we want 'is boys. My husband's name is Dave and my name is Bev. We been chasin' 'em from New York and we think they's here."

I sed, "I ain't seen 'im, but he don't live here. He lives 'bout 5 miles down the road." Then I asked, "Y'all had anythin' to eat?

They said, "No."

I seen that the ice man had a bucket of ice water in 'is hands. So I hollerd for Bill. He come out from behind the ice house and the ice man pitched that water all over 'im. We all laughed. Bill walked over, drippin' wet, to see what I called 'im for. I told 'im to go tell 'is Aunt Sally to fix 2 meals, and bring 'em some tea with some ice.

Bill sed, "I ain't gonna get no ice, 'cause if'n Bob catches me, he'll skin my hide." So I told 'im I'd get the ice.

I went over to the ice house and rung the bell. Well, I got a bucket of water thrown on me. I jist laughed, but Bob looked scared. I told 'im not to worry 'bout it. I were wet head to toe, but it were a warm day, and I'd dry afore long.

Bill brought out the lunches. They had some of 'em smoked mullets, black-eyed peas, cracklin' cornbread and some sweet taters. They et it up. I told Bill to saddle up my horse, and he jist looked at me and asked why I were all wet. They all laughed.

After they et they wanted to know what they owed us. I thought of Ray who always told me, "Don't never be greedy," so I told 'em it were free.

I asked 'im 'bout their pistols. They shore was purty. "Can y'all shoot them through one of 'em oranges if'n I throw it in the air?" I threw the orange in the air and he grabbed that pistol and BAM! That there orange blowed up.

He sed, "Throw another one."

I were lookin' at 'im, but Bev grabbed 'er pistol, and BAM! That orange blowed up.

She sed, "Y'all want to try it?"

I sed, "Shore." She threw the orange and I shot at it, but when I missed and it hit the water, she shot it and blowed it all to pieces.

I sed, "I wish I could shoot like that."

But they sed, "Y'all do. Y'all killed all 'em crooks."

Now, how did everybody hear 'bout that?

We loaded up and Bill wanted to go, too, but I told 'im he couldn't go this time. I told Dave we would go through the woods 'cause it were quicker. He stopped at the store to thank Sally for the food. It were good. They were a small trail through the woods that not many knowed 'bout. We got to Mr. Wall's house, and there he were, sittin' on 'is porch, smokin' 'is pipe with rabbit tobacco in it.

I sed, "Mr. Wall, this here are a G-Man. She are, too."

He sed, "It's 'bout my boys?"

Dave sed, "Yes, it is."

Mr. Wall sed, "I don't know what happened, but I guess y'all's after 'em for somethin' they done. They was here 'bout a week ago, and sed they was goin' to Cuba. I don't know if'n they did or not, but if'n I were lookin' for 'em, I'd go to Tampa. They always go there. It's called, "Ybor City" in Tampa. Try not to kill 'em."

Dave looked at 'im and sed, "I'll do everythin' I can not to shoot 'em."

I seen Mr. Wall cry. I told Dave I had to go back home, and if'n they wanted to go with me, they could spend the night with us. He looked at 'is wife and she agreed. So we went back through the swamp.

The next mornin' they got ready to go. I seen in 'is face it were gonna be hard. A week later, they were a big shoot out south of Tampa. The G-man got shot, but not bad, and the other G-man kilt Mr. Wall's boys. My heart were broken for Mr. Wall.

Taxes

Chapter 23

I got up early. It were 'bout 5:30. That's when the boats leave, and I go set on the dock to watch 'em go. My eye caught somethin'.

I hollered, "Hey, bring that boy back." Bill done slipped out of the house again. "Oh, just take 'im on, but make 'im work." I'm thinkin', *Bill does this jist to see if'n he can do it.*

'Bout dark the boat come back in. Bill were asleep. "Jist let 'im sleep here all night."

Them skeeters will eat 'im up at night. I went in and put my night clothes on. Afore long I heard the door open. It were Bill. He went in and crawled in 'is bed. I didn't tell Sam what I were gonna do. Bill were gonna scrub the deck all through the unwanted fish, and pick up the scraps. But I knowed he were jist wore out. So I thought I'd jist go lay down with 'im. When I woke up he were lookin' at me and sed, "Y'all are a good dad, and I love y'all. Someday I'm gonna make y'all real proud of me."

I looked up the road and seen this ole short man with one of 'em funny-lookin' hats. Think they call 'em a derby. I shore don't want one of 'em. He walked on down to the dock. I were settin' there watchin' the boats come and go. He sed, "My name's Earl. I work for the government. I collect taxes."

I sed, "What's taxes?"

He sed, "We charge y'all money for what y'all own."

Well, I told 'im, "I bought this with my own money, and ain't a gonna give y'all money for what I paid for. When did this here tax start?"

He sed, "This year." He done made me mad, so I sed, "Well, I ain't gonna pay."

He argued, "Yes, y'all are!"

I looked at 'im and sed, "Y'all ever been buried in the ground? Well, if'n y'all don't leave, y'all will be." I could see in 'is eyes that he were scared.

He got up and left on a slow horse. In 'bout an hour he were back with the sheriff and another feller with a gun. I knowed the sheriff, and I liked 'im. The sheriff sed, "Red, y'all can't do what y'all jist did."

I told 'im, "But he wanted to take some of my money."

Earl sed," If'n I wanted to, I could whip y'all's behind."

The sheriff looked at Earl and sed, "Y'all know, he's Red Fussell, and he's the one that kilt all them bad fellers 'round here."

Earl's eyes got real big. He sed, "I didn't mean nothin'."

So the sheriff told me to let 'im do 'is job and check 'round, so I agreed. Earl handed me a bill for 12 dollars. To keep from causin' trouble, I jist paid the 12 dollars and Earl left. The sheriff stayed back with me and sed, "When he found out y'all was Red Fussell, he didn't charge y'all very much." We both jist laughed.

I told the sheriff, "Let's git a glass of tea."

The sheriff started to ring the bell for the ice man, but I sed, "Don't do that."

He sed, "Why?" He rung it anyway. Out come Bob with a bucket of water and throwed it all over the sheriff. I laughed and explained that my son rings the bell all the time, and then he runs to the back of the shed. The ice man run to the back of the shed this time, when he seen it were the sheriff. But then when he seen me laugh, he knowed it were fine.

Shine

Chapter 24

Them Cason boys been makin' shine ever since I can 'member. They make it in the swamp. I never drunk none, so I don't care what they done out there. They raised blue ribbon cane, that's the best crop. Then they made s'rup and sugar out of it. They raised a big corn field and some other crops. Sometimes they raised hell, too, but they was good boys. Only they done made lots of shine. They had a big ole boat and would take all the shine to Tampa, where they'd get a better price.

But the revenuers got wind of where it were comin' from, and had a man and 'is wife, Hal and Peg, come out. Peg could smell a still 10 miles away. And she found a bunch of them. So they come to find the still that were in Homosassa swamp. They come to ask me, but I told 'em I don't drink, so I don't mess with it. Well, Peg put on 'er wadin' boots and a skeeter net over her hat, and she were gonna find it.

Them Cason boys knowed who Hal and Peg was. So they thought they would throw Peg's nose off a bit, and built a big fire in the sand swamp. They put on a drum of ole mash and jist let'er boil. Y'all could smell it real good, but to get in the sand swamp, y'all had to wade water and mud. It were jist bad.

They started out, and she smelt that mash cookin'. They called in 4 more revenuers and they waded all day long. When they got to the drum it were done burnt dry. Well, I knowed they'd done been set up.

The Mullet Boys

By then 'em boys had moved their still and quit cookin'. They hauled the last load down to Tampa.

Hal and Peg and the 4 others come out the next day, and they was et up with them red bugs and skeeters. They was muddy head to toe, and they was real mad at 'em boys. The boys hid their still in Inverness in a barn, but none of us knowed that. One of them revenuer guys looked at me and he sed, "If'n y'all don't tell me where that still is, I'll shoot a hole in y'all's boat!"

I looked at 'im and sed, "Y'all shoot my boat and I'll shoot y'all in y'all's foot."

But Peg sed, "Now, we don't do nothin' like that. If'n y'all know where it is, jist tell us."

But I told 'er I didn't know, and I really didn't know.

They knowed 'em Cason boys was runnin' that still, so they would watch for 'em. The Cason boys took off to the swamp on the river side. They was jist playin' with 'em revenuers. Them revenuers followed 'em all day long. Well, late in the day, them boys come out of the woods carryin' 3 jugs. Them revenue guys run up and grabbed 'em. "Now, we caught y'all!!"

But them boys jist laughed and sed, "These here's water jugs."

So one of the revenue guys tasted it. "They's right. It are water!!"

Peg and Hal sed, "Let's jist go home. We been here long enough." They git ready to leave, and I handed Peg a note to take to my brother. She knowed 'im.

Them Cason boys moved their still back in the swamp. They really was good boys, but they's jist full of mischief. Later the boys learnt they'd been turned in by Homer, the man down the road from 'em. They done stole 'is hogs and sold 'em. So the law come and got 'em.

Big Storm

Chapter 25

I got up the next day. The weather didn't look so good. Mt. Atz
come by and I sed, "Look west. Shore looks bad." All the boats was in
Texas, except for the mullet boat. I told, Bob, the ice man, to take the
boat inside to the river. He sed he'd stay with it.

I told Sam, "I think we better go somewhere. Looks real bad."

I went to the restaurant and told Sally, "I think we's in for a big
blow; y'all gotta leave with us."

We loaded up the Model T and I told Bill to go git Mr. and Mrs. Atz,
and we'd all go together. The Atz's didn't wanna go, but I loaded 'em up
anyway. Our car were real full.

When we left it were rainin' and the wind were blowin' hard. Even
though the Model T were real full, it run good.

We went to Inverness, but there warn't no place for all of us to stay.
Sally wanted to git out at a friend's house and wait out the storm. So
we pulled up to her friend's house and Sally ran to the door. Her friend
welcomed 'er in.

I turned to Sam and sed, "Let's jist go on to Okahumpka to Judy's
house." Sam agreed. An hour later we was there, and the rain were
comin' harder, and the wind were a blowin' real bad. We got the kids
and everyone into Judy's house. It were shore a full house, and 'em kids

got louder and louder.

Finally Sam sed, "Shut y'all's mouth!" They done it. She had a way with kids. I took the boys and went to the barn, and we jist slept there. I 'member when we moved to Homosassa, we slept in a barn. I guess all of 'em back there's dead, if'n they stayed for this storm.

The wind were real bad, but the barn were in good shape, so we was safe. I wondered how things was in Homosassa. If'n they were a double tide it'd be real bad. But there warn't nothin' I could do 'bout it.

It blowed for 3 days, and then the sun come out. I told the boys to clean up the barn. They's old enough now to do good work. I 'member when Lewis and I done that on our way out to Homosassa.

Then we loaded up the Model T. I needed to fill up with gas, so we stopped in Beville's Corner. They had a gas pump with a hand pump. So I filled the Model T with gas and we headed back to Homosassa.

When we crossed the Withlacoochee River, I knowed we was in trouble. But we would make it one way or another.

When we got near Homosassa, they was trees down everywhere, and houses done blown down. I told Sam, "Bet everythin' we had are gone." But as we drove in, it warn't as bad as I thought it'd be. The house were still there. The store were there, and Sally were back and cleanin' it up already. Mr. Atz's house were there, too.

The boat were not at the dock. I thought Bob would have the boat back by now; then it hit me where Bob put it. So I went up the road and seen the boat up on the ground. The tide had been real high. They was people out puttin' boats back in the water. I asked everyone 'round, "Where's Bob?" They all jist looked at me and sed that they didn't know.

So I called the sheriff, and he sed there warn't much no one could do. I guess Bob were somewhere out there in the Gulf. I shore wish I hadna left 'im there. I don't even know where he come from, or where he lived. He jist come by one day and asked me for a job. He were a good worker.

The days jist git shorter and shorter. I miss that ice man. My boys shore give 'im a hard time. Some people sed he were crazy, but I don't think so. He were good at the icehouse.

Sandy and Clem

Chapter 26

Sandy and Clem lived not too far from us. We could see their house along the water. I were settin' at the dock and seen John slippin' in the woods back of Sandy and Clem's house. Then I seen that young red-headed girl go to the barn to feed their horses. In 'bout 3 minutes out come John out the back door, and Carla come out the front. I jist smiled. Both 'em was 14.

I bet anythin' she kissed 'im and 'is heart tingled jist like mine done when I got my first kiss from Sam.

John walked up to the dock and sed, "Dad, can I use the Model T next Saturday?"

I asked 'im, "Where y'all goin'?"

And he sed, "To the picture show in Inverness."

So I sed, "Shore, if'n you don't drive too fast." He'd been driving all over, and every place he went, he done good. Well, he didn't have no license, but the police wouldn't stop 'im if'n he didn't go fast.

I sed, "Who you gonna take?"

He sed, "I hope Carla."

I told 'im he had to ask 'er mama first, but he told me he were scared to.

He sed, "What if'n I ask 'er and she says, 'No'?"

I told 'im he'd jist have to do somethin' else.

The Mullet Boys

I were watchin' that way out on the dock. Monday were wash day, and 'em older girls done the washin'. Sandy pumped 2 tubs of water, one wash pot, and one rinse tub. When 'em girls come in from school and done their homework, they scrubbed the clothes on the scrub-board, and put 'em in the rinse water. The youngest girl hung the clothes on the clothes line. She were jist 9 years old. When they had 'em all hung on the line, they took a pole and raised it up so the clothes wouldn't touch the ground.

Then Sandy built a fire under the wash pot to clean Clem's clothes. He wore 'em close to 3 or 4 days in a row on the railroad, and they was real dirty. He'd been layin' track in the Green Swamp. He only got to come home on the weekend. She'd take 'is clothes from the wash pot and put 'em in the rinse water. Then she'd hang 'em up to dry.

When the washin' were done, they'd take the wash water and scrub the floor. By then the dark clothes would be dry outside. So Sandy built a fire in the wood stove. They had 3 ironin' boards. Them girls ironed all 'em clothes, but not the underwear. I heard one of the girls say their dad made their mom mad one day, and she starched 'is underwear in heavy sugar water and ironed 'em! Guess he musta had a bad week in Green Swamp that week!

James Carlton Fussell

I asked the girls how Sandy got 'er name. The girls told me, "When she were a little girl, they lived over on the sand hills. Her dad made 'er a sand box, and whenever anybody come by, she'd throw sand at 'em. They say that 'er mama put a switch to 'er, but when 'er mama walked away, she'd throw sand at 'er, too. I don't know if'n all that's true or not, but it shore sounds like 'er." We all laughed.

When Clem come home on the weekend, she told 'im, "You ain't comin' in this house that dirty." So he had to take a bath in the horse trough out in the barn. If'n it were cold he shore didn't wanna do that, but he done it anyway. She fed 'im real good. He shore did like apple pie on Friday nights. He could eat the whole pie. And he were a good dad to 'is girls. Every time he come home, he'd bring the girls somethin', jist some little gift. They looked forward to it.

On Saturday they raked the yard and put the trash in the ditch back behind the house. That boy of mine would slip out back to get a kiss, and the two younger girls wouldn't tell on 'er. John told Carla he were gonna go ask 'er mama if'n she could go to Inverness to the picture show.

So he went to 'er house and took off 'is shoes 'cause he knowed she kept 'er house real clean. She told 'im to come in. Clem were sittin' in 'is chair with 'is shoes off. Nobody had shoes on. He shore were glad he done took 'is off, too.

He told 'er that 'is name were John Fussell, who had the shrimp boats. And he sed, "What I'd like to know is if'n I could take Carla to Inverness to the picture show."

He were a shakin' standin' there waitin' for 'er to answer. She looked at 'im so long he thought she were gonna shoot 'im. Finally she sed, "I think y'all are too young to go to Inverness to the picture show.

His heart jist fell. He were afraid she'd yell at 'im, but she didn't. She jist looked at 'im and sed, "If'n y'all was older, I might let 'er go."

He jist politely sed, "Thank y'all". He told 'em he had to go, and he looked over at Carla. She jist smiled at 'im. That made 'im feel good.

I were settin' on the dock, and John set down next to me. He sed, "Dad, I asked Mrs. Sandy if'n Carla could go to the picture show, but she told me if'n we was older she might think 'bout it.

Well, I looked at 'im and seen myself when I were 'is age and in love, so I sed, "Don't give up." He asked me what he should do, and I told 'im, "When you see 'em girls rakin' the yard, go help 'em." He jist looked at me.

The week passed fast and the shrimp boats was a comin' to the dock. Bill and I was jist settin' on the dock, and Bill sed, "What's John doin'?" John had a sack and he were goin' on the boat. I sed, "I bet he's gonna git some of 'em shrimp."

Bill started to git up, but I told 'im to let John git some shrimp. Sed, "I'm shore we won't miss the few he gits."

Bill asked me what he were gonna do with the shrimp, and I told 'im, "You know that red-headed girl over there at Sandy's house? Well, he's in love with 'er." We both laughed.

John went down the road to Carla's house. He knocked on the door. Sandy answered the door. He handed 'er the bag of shrimp and sed, "Here's some shrimp for y'all's dinner tonight."

Sandy looked at 'im and smiled at 'im. Then she began 'memberin' jist how she felt when she were in young love with Clem, and sed, "Thank y'all, John."

John sed, "Y'all are welcome." He felt real good.

Saturday come 'round and the girls was out rakin'. When John seen 'em, he got 'is rake and went to help 'em. It didn't take long with all of them rakin'. They put the trash in the ditch. John and Carla slipped behind the barn to get a kiss, and each time John's heart would flutter.

Carla fixed lunch, but sed, "We don't have no ice, so we won't have no ice tea."

John sed, "I'll go get some ice."

He went home to git a bucket of ice from the ice house. He knowed not to ring the bell 'cause he didn't wanna git wet. He jist opened the door.

We had to find a new ice man, after we lost Bob and so we hired Gene. Gene were a drifter and he were hungry. He done stopped by the restaurant lookin' for a job. So we hired 'im to work the ice house.

Gene told John, "Jist take what y'all want." And Gene picked up a bucket that Bob used to throw water on them boys. He learned real fast 'bout what Bob done to the boys when they rang the bell. John knowed Gene could beat 'im to the door 'cause he were closer. So John grabbed a bucket and run as fast as he could. Gene acted like he were gonna throw water on 'im, but the bucket were empty. I were settin' outside watchin' and laughed so hard. So did the ice man. John laughed too, and then went back and filled the bucket with ice. He went back to Mrs. Sandy's house. They had ice tea. She put the rest of the ice in the ice box.

Sandy told 'em girls to go to their bedrooms. She had somethin' to tell John, but she warn't gonna tell 'em. When John went home he were jist as happy as he could be.

The girls washed and ironed clothes on Friday. They washed windows on Saturday and raked leaves. John didn't help this time. He were busy checkin' out the Model T. He checked the oil, the tires, the water and cleaned the car up real good. And it looked real good too. Then he filled it with gas. Saturday 'bout noon he fired up the Model T and went to get Carla. Bill and I was settin' on the dock. We laughed at what we seen. There went that Model T with John and Carla in the front, and Mrs. Sandy were ridin' in the rumble seat! They all looked happy. Mrs. Sandy and Carla never seen a picture show afore.

They got to the picture show place, and John bought the tickets and a bag of popcorn. They all watched 'em cowboys shoot everybody. When it were over, they walked to the Model T and started the drive home. Carla set next to John again. He were really in love.

They got home 'bout dark. When they got out of the Model T, Mrs. Sandy thanked 'im and quietly sed, "Y'all can kiss 'er." His heart were jist a beatin' so fast he thought it would blow up. After he kissed 'er, he drove home and didn't think the tires was even touchin' the ground.

The next day, I told John to wash down 'em shrimp boats; they was goin' to Texas if'n the weather were good. They left on Friday, and John asked if'n he could use the Model T again. I sed, "Shore. Where you goin'?"

He sed, "I want to take Carla and her sister to the picture show." He had done checked with Mrs. Sandy and asked Mr. Clem, too, if'n he wanted to go. But he sed he had to get ready to go back to work. Mrs. Sandy sed he could take Carla and 'er sister this time. They was so happy they hardly talked.

Saturday they went to Inverness. They got there on time, and John paid their way to the picture show. Mrs. Sandy give 'em money to pay, but John paid it anyway. Them cowboys and Indians shore shot a lot of shells. They had a box of popcorn and got a candy bar too. My! It shore were good!

When they got back home Mrs. Sandy were lookin' out the window. But Carla kissed 'im anyway, and so did 'er little sister. John loved 'em all. He went home and put the Model T in the shed, after it were gassed up again.

John went inside and learned they was 'bout to have bad weather off the coast of Texas, so the shrimp boats done gone inland to get out of the bad weather and come home. We had to ship the shrimp we already had to New York, so Carla come to the fish house to help John put shrimp in the barrels. It ain't a clean job neither.

It were 'bout dark and John sed, "Let's go get somethin' to eat." So they went down to the fish house. Carla never et in a fish house afore, so she told John to order for 'er. He ordered smoked mullet, grits with butter, beans and a soda water. She never had one of them afore neither, and she like it all.

John sed he'd walk 'er home, but I walked in and told 'em that if'n they'd wait a little bit, I'd have some smoked mullet they could take.

I were back afore long, and John and Carla walked to Carla's house. She opened the door and sed, "Mama, my boyfriend's here with some smoked mullet." She come to the door, but she were cryin'."

They'd been a shootin' over at Green Swamp, but they don't know who got shot. So John run home and told me, "I need the Model T to go to Green Swamp."

I jist sed, "That's fine."

John and Sandy left the girls at the house. It were 'bout dark, but John knowed the way. I shore hoped it weren't Clem that got shot. I told John to take the shot gun with buckshot shells, jist in case he needed 'em. It were 'bout 30 miles away. They got there in 'bout an hour and they were a big fire goin' near where the men stayed. When they drove up they seen Clem, so they knowed he were fine.

Afore they left, John pulled out some smoked mullet and give to Clem. Clem told 'em he shot a man for stealin' railroad stuff, and they took the man to jail in Dade City.

As they left Green Swamp, they were a panther with 'er kittens right in the middle of the road. John sed, "It would be a shame to shoot 'em." But finally the panther run to the woods and 'er kittens followed. He were shore glad they was gone.

James Carlton Fussell

John stopped at a gas station and got 'em a soda pop to drink on the way and got back home afore long. John opened the door for Sandy, and she sed, "Thank y'all. Y'all are a good boy, and I'm glad y'all're my girl's boyfriend." Then she kissed 'im on the cheek.

Jist like I told 'im, sometimes it takes time.

(Without the real Sandy today, this book would never a-been wrote. Thank y'all. Red Fussell)

Smoke mullet

Do not Take the scale of flay on side Take the fin out Leave the back bone on one side. Salt and pepper make sure you smoker is hot place Charcoal on The bottom with A pan of water Above place The mullet fish side up scale side down cook Till they dry out some will Take Longer it About the size.

Fire on the Boat

Chapter 27

It were a long day. It rained 'bout all day. John had been cleanin' the boats and made shore they was all gassed up, and he checked the water supply. I spent most of the day in the restaurant and brought home food for Sam. She warn't feelin' so good.

I started to put on my night clothes and seen John out the window run for the flat boat. Here come Bill too. I knowed somethin' were up. So I grabbed my shoes and put 'em on. I run out the door to the dock. Then I seen why they was runnin'. They were a boat on fire out there. I seen John and Bill go through Hell's Gate, left, 2 rights, 2 lefts, right, as fast as they could go, but knowed it would take 'em 'bout half an hour to git to there. I shore hoped they could save the people on board, but it didn't look good.

The flat bottom boat were the fastest boat we had. I looked 'round and they were a bunch of people to help too, if'n they could. Sam's sister, Sally, sed, "I'll go make some coffee." I shore am glad she lives here.

About 2 hours later I seen the boat come back through Hell's Gate. They pulled up to the dock. They was 5 people in the boat and they was cold and wet, so we give 'em some hot coffee.

Sandy sed, "Come on to my house and we'll dry your clothes." She made 'em take off their clothes, and the girls ironed the wet clothes till they was dry. The people sat by the stove to git warm.

When they was warm, Sam's sister, Sally told 'em to come and get somethin' to eat. One of the men sed, "I would pay y'all, but we lost it all in the fire." Sam's sister told 'em not to worry 'bout it.

We was settin' in the restaurant when one of the men sed, "I need a car. We need to get to Tampa as soon as possible." I told 'em I could loan 'em mine, and they could drop it off at Lewis' Fish Camp. We could run the boat down to git it. I told John to go gas it up and to check the oil and tires.

The man looked at me real funny and sed, "I never thought people would do that for someone."

Then they told Bill and John they was 2 metal boxes in the sunken boat, and asked if'n they would see if'n they could find 'em. They wasn't heavy, and they was sealed up good. The boys agreed to go back to the boat and look.

Some time later when the mailman come, he brought a letter from Lewis that sed, "Y'all's cars is at my place."

I thought, *Not cars, just car. I sent a letter back to Lewis to tell the men who dropped off the car that we found one of them boxes they wanted, and told 'im we'd bring it down on Friday.*

They was 5 of us in the boat, but it warn't a bad run. We'd jist put a new motor in one of the shrimp boats to see how it would work. It didn't take long afore we pulled into Lewis' dock. His girls shore was glad to see us.

The girls and Lewis knowed where they could find the man that I loaned the Model T to. It warn't long afore he come up in a big car. They was 2 men that stepped out with guns. I were thinkin', *I shore hope they don't shoot us.*

The one man sed, "I jist found out y'all are Red Fussel, the one who got the men that kilt y'all's dad. I don't blame y'all at all."

I give 'im the box and told 'im we hadn't found the other one, but we was still lookin', and if'n we found it, we'd let 'im know.

He sed, "I give that Model T of y'alls to Lewis' girls, but I got y'all a new pickup truck. Lewis told me y'all'd like to have one. And for the girls that ironed our clothes dry, there's a box in the back of the pickup. I'm havin' a new stove sent to Sally. I think she needs it. You don't know how much y'all helped me that night. I told those on the boat we'd probably drown, but here y'all's boys come. I tried to give 'em money, but they wouldn't take it. They's real fine boys."

He got back in the big car and they drove off. Lewis looked at me and sed, "That's the bad person in this county. He would hang anybody that messed with 'im."

I asked Lewis if'n the pickup were out back, and he sed that it were.

Lewis sed, "And he give John and Bill new cars, too." He told me that if anyone in Tampa give me a hard time to let 'im know.

I told Bill and John to come out back. We walked out back and I sed, "Boys, these here are y'all's new cars." That's when my 15 year old's mouth fell wide open. He couldn't even say a word.

Then Lewis laughed. He sed, "He got a new car and don't even have no driver license."

John sed, "I'll jist tell 'em that I'm Red Fussell's son, and they'll let me go."

Then Lewis sed, 'Y'all're right, but it might be to jail!"

We all laughed. Mr. Atz rode down with us in the boat, so I told Mr. Atz that I'd take the boat back and for 'im to ride with the boys, but to not let either of the boys drive too fast. "Them cars need to be broke in, but not fast."

I got back at the dock and they come in 'bout half an hour later. They had a good time with them new cars. I shore like my green truck, too. I told John to take the box down to Sandy's house for them girls. And I went down to see what it were. They was new shoes and even a hat. It's always good to see happy people. They were somethin' for Sandy, too. It were a radio with a battery all wrapped up. She were happier than the girls. She grabbed John and hugged 'im. His face turned as red as a fox's behind in pokeberry season. We all laughed.

It'd been a good day. I stopped in to tell Sam I were back, but she didn't feel good. The next day Bill and John looked for the box in the ocean again. They found it 'bout dark. John wanted to look inside, but I told 'im it warn't ours to look at.

Friday we loaded up and John and I went back to Tampa. We stopped at Lewis' to see if'n he would get in touch with that man. In 'bout 45 minutes he were there with 'em 2 guards. They stepped out with guns. After they looked 'round he got out. I handed 'im the box and told 'im how happy them girls was. He sed he liked to make people happy.

James Carlton Fussell

I told 'em all I needed to git goin', but the man sed, "Don't leave till the stuff I have for y'all gits here. And any time y'all are in Tampa, git in touch with me."

Lewis told me they was a war goin' on in Tampa. They shot and kilt everyone that gits in their way.

In 'bout an hour a truck come with a bunch of boxes, and they sed to load 'em in the pickup. Well, I had to borrow Lewis' trailer. I couldn't git it all in my truck.

We got back afore dark. We stopped at Sandy's house first. They was 3 boxes for them girls and one for Clem. Won't he be surprised with a new Stetson hat! I'd like to keep that, but I don't need it. I don't know what the girls got, but I'm shore they's happy with it. He give Sam's sister a whole set of cast iron pots and pans. I guess one good deed brings another. When we left the stuff at Sandy's house I told John to take it inside.

The Tampa man told the boys they could have anythin' left on that sunken boat. They got a bunch of stuff off it. 'Bout 3 months after the boat sunk, I got a letter from Lewis sayin' someone done kilt that man that give us all this stuff. I guess when y'all live that way, y'all die that way.

Sam's sister got 'er new stove. It shore were a nice stove. I asked Sam if'n she'd like to go see it, but she sed she jist didn't feel up to it.

The Long Line

Chapter 28

I were settin' on the dock one day with Bill and John and asked if'n they'd like to put a long line in the deep water. They sed they could git lots of big fish doin' that. I told 'em I could send a letter to Lewis to tell 'im to git us a line and hooks and told the boys we could kill a wild hog in Swamp Point for bait. They thought they'd like to do that.

So I sent the letter to Lewis and told 'im to git a mile line, some hooks and a reel to wind the line up. I left Monday to go to Lewis' Fishin' Camp to pick it all up. I were goin' through where they was divin' for sponges and looked up. I seen a red light flashin' on a car. So I pulled over and stopped.

The police pulled up and I sed, "What'd I do?"

Then I seen it were one of 'em boys from Homosassa. They shore do grow up fast! He sed, "I jist wanted to say, 'Hi'. I miss the bunch on the river."

So I told 'im that thangs was fine back home. Told 'im the boys and I was fixin' to go long line fishin', and I were headed to git the long line and stuff.

He told me there's some crooks in the Gulf, and they kilt 3 fisher-men jist last week. They's got a real fast boat with lots of guns, so he told me to make shore we take our guns. He went on to say that it were the Smith Shrimp Boat men was the ones they kilt. They jist shot 'em for no reason. They's jist bad people. I thanked 'im for the information, and told 'im I'd watch for 'em.

I left and was on my way to Tampa to see Lewis. I got to 'is dock and knowed right away that somethin' weren't right. Lewis come outside and, he too told me they was some bad people in the Gulf. They kilt 3 people jist last week and 4 today. The Coast Guard were out there lookin' for 'em.

Lewis had the long line, the short line and the spools to wind 'em up ready for me. I paid 'im 160 dollars for the long line and left Tampa. It were startin' to rain, not hard but enough to git me wet. I got back home, and it done stopped rainin', but it were still damp. I stopped at the dock to unload the long line and drove up to the house. I seen John on the way and told 'im to set the hog trap.

The next day there weren't no hog. So John shot an ole bore hog and kilt 'im. He skinned 'im and cut 'im up in small pieces, jist right for a good sized fish. I told John we would put it out tomorrow 'bout 30 miles out in the Gulf.

I got my gun out and cleaned and oiled it, and made shore I had plenty of shells. Then I got the gun I kept on the boat when they were war in the Gulf. I had 'bout 4 shells. I cleaned that gun and put shells in both guns, all they'd hold. I'd rather have more than what I need, than not enough.

We left bout 5 the next mornin'. We et at Sam's sister's place first. Sally always has good meals. Then we headed out to the Gulf.

I told the boys 'bout the crooks and that they had now kilt 7 people. They don't know who they is, except the boat has a green stripe on the side.

We was out close to 30 miles. We took the main line and placed a hook 'bout every 2 feet with some pork on it. We had jist let out 'bout all of the line when we seen a boat with a green stripe on the side. I told the boys, "Now if'n that boat comes up on the side of the boat, lay on the floor. The side of the boat will stop a bullet."

I climbed in the top where they couldn't see me. Even though we had all the line out, I sed, "Let's go home and come back tomorrow." But when we started to leave I seen the boat were comin' up real fast. I sed, "Everybody, git down inside and jist let the boat run. Don't stand up, lay flat." They pulled up side of us and shot at us. There musta been 10 -15 with guns.

Way off in the distance I seen a shrimp boat comin' our way. They leveled up with their machine gun and fired at 'em crooks. I seen some of 'em fall. The others run for the wheel house, so I filled it full of bullets. They tried to make a run for it, but it were too late.

I seen on the other side; it were the Smith Shrimp Boat, and they hit that boat right in the middle and busted it wide open. Them that was still alive was in the water. The boys on the shrimp boat took their guns and shot them not already dead, jist enough for 'em to bleed. That way the sharks would git 'em. I wouldn't a did that, but I don't blame 'em. Them crooks had done kilt 7 of their friends. I'm jist glad it's over.

They pulled their boat up side ours and tied off. Their captain come on board. He thanked me for what I done and sed, "What's y'all's name?"

I sed, "Red Fussell."

He looked me straight in the eye and sed, "If y'all ever need my help, jist call me. What happened here will never be told." He called his crew and told 'em that too. Them crook's boat had sunk to the bottom. Stuff were floatin' out of it. I looked to see if any of them crooks was still there. The sharks was, but not them.

I looked at the boys and sed, "We best pull the long line in. All we're gonna catch is sharks."

They put the reel up and started pullin' in line and hooks. We took the hooks off as the line come in. They was a lot of fish on the line. It were 'bout dark when we got the line in. We had a boat load of fish. We iced down the fish. We'll have to clean and pack 'em tomorrow. The day hadn't been too bad, but it were a sad one.

We parked at the dock and filled the hole with ice. We washed up and went to bed. I didn't wake up till late. John and Bill was runnin' the pump, to pump out the ice. John got Sandy and Carla and 'er other sister to clean the fish and pack 'em. It's hard work, but it pays good.

They had all the fish cleaned and packed in ice and placed in the wooden barrels ready to ship to the market in New York. As close as I could tell it were 'bout 550 dollars worth. Each crew member got 20 dollars, which were good pay for a day. I give the girls 5 dollars and give Sandy 7.50. Not a bad run for a day.

James Carlton Fussell

About 2 months later, the Coast Guard found part of a boat floatin' off the coast of Tampa. It were from Key West. It were missin' for 'bout 3 months. Somebody stole it, and the owner weren't happy 'bout it. I sed to myself, "I bet he owned it and were in on the stealin."

I were sittin' on the dock when a car drove up. A man got out. He were 'bout 60 or 70 in age. He sed, "My name's Rob Smith. That was my boys on the shrimp boat y'all met in the Gulf. I lost one son to 'em killers. I wanna thank y'all for what y'all done."

I jist sed, "We do what we have to do. I don't like it sometimes, but y'all do what y'all think is right."

I asked 'im if'n he had lunch yet today, and he hadn't, so I sed, "Well, let's go eat lunch." We went inside and had some smoked mullet, grits, black-eyed peas, cracklin' cornbread and a big glass of ice tea.

When we finished lunch he sed, "I gotta go, but if'n y'all ever need somethin', let me know, and I'll help y'all in any way I can."

About a week later a man drove up. I were settin' on the dock. He walked to the dock and sed, "My name's Homer Jones. I live in Key West. That were my boat that y'all sunk in the Gulf."

I sed, "I didn't sink it. But what were it doin' out there? I hear they warn't fishin."

He sed, "I guess they was boat ridin'. They warn't doin' nothin' but fishin' and ridin."

But I sed, "I hear tell they was crooks. Did they belong to y'all?" I looked 'im in the eye and then he looked to the ground.

He finally sed, "Yes, they was my boys. Once they was good boys and good fishermen, but they found out that if'n they robbed people, they didn't have to work as much. What I'm here for is to know how they died."

I wanted to tell 'im how they died, but couldn't tell 'im I kilt 'em.

I sed, "They musta drowned, but I ain't shore."

He sed, "Thanks. I guess them sharks et 'em."

I seen a tear come to 'is eyes and wished I could help, but they chose what life they wanted. I watched 'im drive off. I'm shore glad it weren't my boys.

I looked up and here come another car. I thought I seen it afore, but couldn't place it. Then out stepped a little short man with a note book. I knowed who he were then. Earl, the tax collector were back. I started to git my gun and shoot 'im, but they'd put me in jail.

He walked up and sed, "I come to git y'all's tax money."

I sed, "I don't owe no tax money."

He sed, "Do I have to get the law again to git it from y'all?"

I knowed I'd have to pay it anyhow, so might as well pay it now and git it over. So I sed, "Go ahead and tell me how much."

He looked 'round for a while and when he come back, I sed, "Let's go et some lunch."

He jist looked at me like I shot 'im, but sed, "That'll be fine."

We went to Sally's place. She fried up some grouper, baked beans, homemade biskits with some guava jelly, big glass of iced tea and a big ole piece of guava pie. If'n it gits any better than this, I want it, too. We et lunch, and I asked 'im where he were from.

He sed, "Up north."

I asked if'n he were a carpet bagger and he sed that he were, till he went to work for the government.

I asked, "Is it a bad job, if'n y'all don't get shot at?" We both laughed and I asked 'im how much I owed 'im.

He sed, "Jist 20 dollars." I asked if'n I could pay half of it now and half of it later, but he told me I had to pay it all at once.

He weren't a bad feller. He jist had a bad job. I still think they should give that job to a big man, not some little short man.

(Earl is still a good friend to me today.)

James Carlton Fussell

Guava pie
3 Tbsp flour
1/2 c sugar
1 Lime grated
1 Tsp cinnamon
1/4 Tsp nut nutmeg
1/8 Tsp salt
Graham cracker crust
4 c peeled and thinly sliced guavas
1 Tbsp Lime juice
3 Tsb cold butter cut in pieces

set oven 425 degress
mix flour, sugar, grated, Lime cinnamon
nutmet and salt
put guava slices on bottom of crust
sprinkle with flour and sugar mix (can leave
out sugar)
sprinkle with lime juice cut butter pieces
L oven Temperature To 350 degees
Bake 30-40 minutes

Sam

Chapter 29

I got up 'bout 5:30 to see the sun come up in the Gulf. It shore were purty. I went back to the house to looked at Sam. She were jist so sick. I took 'er to Inverness to see the doctor again. I put 'er in the pickup and we left. She begged me not to take 'er, but I did hope they could do some good. We got to Inverness in no time, and she seen the doctor.

After she seen the doctor, I took 'er outside to the truck, and I went back inside to talk to the doctor. He told me 'er heart were real bad, and she may live a week, or a month, but not much longer. I wanted to cry, but I didn't. My heart were jist broken. All I ever wanted were Sam, and now she's gonna die, and I can't do nothin' 'bout it.

I stopped by the lumber yard and bought some good wood. Sam asked me what the lumber were for. I jist told 'er I were gonna build somethin'.

When we got back home I told Bill to put the lumber up for me, and I lifted Sam and put 'er in the flat boat.

She sed, "Where we goin'?"

I told 'er, "Shell Island."

She sed she'd like that, and she leaned against me. I put my arm 'round 'er and we pulled up to Shell Island.

She sed, "I kissed y'all the first time right here."

James Carlton Fussell

I sed, "Y'all shore did."

She told me she wanted to be buried here where we dug up the gold, and I told 'er, then, that were what I wanted, too. We set there 'bout 30 minutes and she sed, "I wanna go home. I know I'm gonna die soon. That's what the doctor told me. I jist don't wanna leave y'all."

When we got back to the dock Bill carried 'er to the house. I asked 'im to build a box to put 'er in, and told 'im that were what the lumber were for. Then I went to see a man who would jist bill me for makin' an air tight metal box to put the wooden box in. And I told 'im to make 2 of 'em. In 'bout a week I had the boxes and he billed me for them.

I told Bill that Sam wanted to be buried on Shell Island. And I told 'im that were where we dug up the gold, and I wanted to put a piece of gold in 'er hand afore we buried 'er. But I didn't want nobody to know where she were buried. I told 'im I wanted to be buried there, too.

I seen Sam gittin' worse every day. I went home 'bout 5:30. She shore felt bad. I put my night clothes on, and Sam come in and set down beside me. She sed, "You ole red-headed boy; I've always loved y'all. I need to know somethin'. Would y'all take that Model T we had, or would y'all take me now?"

I told 'er, "That ain't even a fair question."

She jist laughed and leaned against me. It shore felt good. Then I noticed she hadn't moved for a while, and she had quit breathin'. I knowed she were gone. I jist laid 'er on the couch. She looked at peace.

I got dressed again and walked down to where Bill were at and told 'im 'is mama were gone. He sed, "I'll git the truck and we can take 'er to the doctor."

But I told 'im, "It will do no good. She's already gone. I need for y'all to dig 'er grave." Through 'is tears, he told me he'd have it done the next day.

I had the sheriff come and look at 'er and to call Sam's sister, Judy, in Okahumpka and tell 'er, "We'll bury 'er on Friday."

He sed he'd do it. Then I seen the mailman that went to Tampa and asked 'im to tell Lewis, that Sam died, and we'll bury 'er on Friday.

I tried to pay 'im, but he sed, "No. If'n I asked y'all's boys to do any-thin' for me, they'd jist do it."

I told John to bring the box to the house and put it on the table. I took them silk table cloths, and got Sam's sister to put 'er weddin' dress on 'er. She were havin' a real hard time. She closed the shop down, and then she opened it back up for the people to go eat.

I put Sam in the box like I seen my dad do. Judy, from Okahumpka, come on Thursday. They had a big crowd comin' in a boat and they brought lots of food with 'em. Sally cooked a bunch of food, too.

I put a gold coin in Sam's hand and closed 'er hand. Lewis come on Friday mornin'. His wife stayed home. Lewis' 3 girls come with 'im with 2 little boys.

Friday mornin' come, but it didn't git no easier. About 10:30 we had the funeral and had a grave marker. The men of the neighborhood done painted the church inside and out. It looked real good.

The funeral were over, so I told John to git somebody to load 'er in the box and to bolt it tight. Then we loaded it in the back of the shrimp boat.

John sed, "Y'all gonna put 'er in the Gulf?"

I sed, "Y'all'll know some day."

When they had 'er on the back of the boat, I started the boat. John wanted to go too, but I sed, "No, this is somethin' I gotta do alone."

I went through Hell's Gate, left, 2 rights, 2 lefts, right, and headed out in the Gulf, turned left, and pulled up to Shell Island. The hole were already dug. I took the boom, hooked it to the metal box, and lifted it into the hole. I eased it down and then filled the hole in. It shore were a long night. I put some brush over it so nobody would know she were buried there, and brought the boom back on the boat. I told Sam I'd be back to see 'er. Then I jist cried all the way back to the dock. But she were in no pain now.

Lewis were at the dock when I got back. He wanted to know if'n I needed anythin'. But I told 'im, "No. I'm okay."

He sed he had to git back to Tampa 'cause they had a big shipment of fish comin'.

I told 'im, "I understand. I'll see y'all real soon. Y'all have a real good family."

Lewis' girls all worked hard, and both of Sam's sisters worked hard to keep everybody fed. I wrote Sally a check for 500 dollars for feedin' all them people. She looked at it and jist threw it in the trash. I looked at 'er, and she sed, "Don't y'all say a word. When I needed help y'all took me in. Now it's my turn."

James Carlton Fussell

The boys was leavin' to fish long line for a few days and asked me to go, but I didn't wanna go. I thought I'd jist go to Tampa for a few days.

On the way to Tampa, I looked up, and there were a flashin' red light, so I stopped. The kid from Homosassa walked up to the truck. He sed, "Mr. Fussell, I jist stopped y'all to say, 'I'm real sorry Sam died.'" I knowed how much y'all loved 'er. That bad bunch in the Gulf are gone. Everybody knowed who got rid of 'em crooks, and everybody's real glad." He sed, "Tell John I sed, 'Hi'".

I sed, "Come see us sometime." And he left.

I started out, but somethin' jist don't seem quite right when I talked with that policeman. So I turned 'round and stopped 'im. I sed, "Tell me what's really goin' on with y'all. What's wrong?"

He looked at me with tears in 'is eyes. "My dad's real sick, and he may die at any time."

I sed, "Is they anythin' I can do?"

He sed, "No. I jist needed someone to talk to."

I sed, "Come on. I'll buy y'all's lunch."

But he sed he couldn't 'cause he needed to git back to work.

The Ring

Chapter 30

I jist took my shoes off when I heard the shrimp boat blow the horn, 2 short, 1 long. I knowed who that were, that red-headed boy of mine. I seen Carla runnin' to the dock. Every time I seen 'em together it makes me happy. They's so in love. I seen her run to the boat and give 'im a big hug, then a kiss. Tears come to my eyes. I shore miss Sam.

They stood there 'bout 10 minutes. Then I heard 'er scream and run for the house. I seen John standin' there with a big smile, and I thought, *What's he done now?*

I put my shoes back on. I had to go find out what he done. I went down where John were puttin' ice on the shrimp so they wouldn't spoil. I sed, "John, what'd y'all do to Carla?"

He jist laughed.

I sed, "It ain't funny."

He sed, "Go ask 'er."

So I went to Sandy and Clem's house and knocked on the door. Sandy come to the door.

I sed, "What's John done to make Carla so unhappy?"

She jist laughed, and I sed, "I jist don't like this one bit." I were mad, but Carla come to the door. I shore do like her. I sed, "What's my son done to y'all?"

She jist smiled and sed, "Look at my finger. He give me a ring! I can't wait to get married. Not now, but I'll marry that red-headed boy some day."

Sandy come over and sed, "What do y'all think 'bout that?"

I sed, "I were 'bout to get real mad when everybody were laughin' and I didn't know why." I knowed they was in love, and I were happy for 'em.

They unloaded the shrimp. John had a real good haul, but one of them boats didn't do so good. They made some money, but not what they should of. John sed he thought it were 'cause them on the other boat wouldn't listen to what he told 'em to do. He thought it were 'cause he were so young. So I told John I'd talk to 'im.

I went to see 'im and sed, 'John's in charge all them boats, so y'all gotta do what he says."

The man looked at me and sed, "He ain't even dry behind the ears yet. He won't tell me what to do."

I sed, "Well, if'n that's the way y'all feel, jist leave."

He sed, "Y'all ain't nothin' but a bunch of thieves, Fussell."

And I told 'im again to leave.

He sed, "What if'n I don't? I can whip a shrimp like y'all."

I told 'im that I could hire somebody to whip 'im everyday, but that wouldn't do no good and again I told 'im to go!

He sed, "Do I get my pay?"

Then I looked at 'im real hard and asked 'im, "They's somethin' botherin' y'all. What's really wrong?"

He sed, "My wife's gonna die, and I can't save 'er. And I don't have no money to take 'er to Tampa and have the operation that would cure 'er."

So I told 'im to have 'er ready 'bout 6 in the mornin' and we'd take 'er to Tampa.

He jist said, "I can't. I ain't got no money."

I looked at 'im and sed, "I do. Jist have 'er ready and out by the boat at 6."

I picked both of 'em up the next mornin'. She were so sick and hurtin'. We arrived at Tampa General. The doctor checked 'er out and sed 'er gall bladder were bad, and sed it cost 200 dollars to remove it.

I sed, "Do I pay y'all after the surgery or up front?"

The doctor looked at me and sed, "Ain't y'all Red Fussell?"

I sed, "I shore am."

The doctor sed that 'is son were kilt on Smith's Shrimp Boat.

I told 'im that bunch was a bad bunch.

But he sed, "But y'all was the one that took care of it."

The doctor told us that she'd be there for 'bout a week.

I told 'im, "This here man's my friend. I give 'im some money so he could eat and get a room. When I git back to pick 'em up, I'll pay the bill."

He sed, "That'll be fine."

The week went by real quick. I drove back to Tampa. She shore looked better. I brought John's car so she'd have more room.

We left Tampa, and in 'bout an hour we'd be home. The man asked me, "How much did the doctor charge?"

I sed, "Don't worry 'bout it."

But he sed, "I'll pay it all back. Jist tell me how much."

When we drove up to 'is house 'is little girl, 'bout 7 years old, come runnin' out and sed, "Did my mama die?"

I almost cried. To think, if'n that doctor hadn't operated on 'er she'd be dead. Her daddy sed, "If'n it weren't for Mr. Fussell, y'all's mama would be dead."

She run over and hugged me 'round the neck and sed, "Thank y'all."

Then he looked at me and sed, "You ain't as big as nothin', but y'all's heart's as big as this here car! Can I come back to work?"

I sed, "Y'all shore can, but y'all gotta remember who's the boss."

He sed, "I'll be there tomorrow and I'll be a good worker."

John asked me if'n he should fire 'im. I sed, "No, he were jist havin' a bad time." I told John that he'd be a good worker from here on, and if'n he didn't do as he was told, to let 'im go.

The next day he showed up and he handed me a box. He sed, "My 7 year old made y'all some cookies." They was good, and I shared 'em with Sally, Sam's sister.

Them boats was gone 3 days, and then I heard 2 short and 1 long blast. There goes that red-headed girl. I watched as she hugged 'is neck and kissed 'im. I asked John "How'd he do?"

He replied, "Best man I got!"

Bill Left

Chapter 31

I got up as the sun come up. I had no Sam, and guess I'll never git over it. I et at Sally's. She shore were a good cook. Then I left, walked down to the dock and set down on the bench. I seen Bill comin'. He set down and sed, "I gotta tell y'all and John somethin'. I jist told one of them boys that hang 'round the dock, to tell John to come up to our dock so I can tell y'all at the same time."

In jist a little bit, John showed up. Bill sed, "Have a seat, John."

"This is what I'm gonna do. I'm gittin' married next month to Sarah. They own the ranch east of Inverness, and I'll be runnin' the ranch and buildin' a house. So, what I'm gonna do is give all them boats here to John." John's mouth jist couldn't say a word.

I looked at Bill and sed, "We can pay y'all for y'all's part."

But he sed, "I don't want no pay, but a mess of fish would be good once in a while."

Bill sed, "Sarah's dad jist bought another 2,000 acreas for the cattle ranch. It's gonna be one of the biggest ranches in Florida. John, I may even let y'all ride my horse. And then he laughed. I'll miss my boat, but I'm in love with Sarah, and they need me to run the ranch. She don't have no brothers or sisters, so it's up to us to keep the ranch goin'. If'n y'all git tired of fishin' I'll give y'all a job on the ranch."

John finally sed, "I'm not shore I can run them boats alone."

Bill sed, "Shore y'all can. Y'all've been doin' it."

I sed, "I'm happy for y'all. Will we be able to come to the weddin'?"

He sed, "Yes, and y'all can come to the ranch any time."

The month passed real quick, and they had the weddin' in the church at Inverness. Sarah shore were purty. I were real happy for Bill, but I thought of Sam and missed 'er. Sarah's dad done give them a new car for a weddin' present.

I felt good. I got 2 real good boys.

I looked at John. There were that red-headed girl with 'im. She were dressed up and looked good, too. She looked like 'er mama. All the girls did. I could see that John were in love. It won't be long till they git married, too. I bet 'em 2 red-heads will breathe fire sometimes.

Bill left on 'is honeymoon and we come back to the Gulf. I looked out at the Gulf and walked out on the dock. I climbed in the flat boat and went out through Hell's Gate, left, 2 rights, 2 lefts, right, and headed to Shell Island. I pulled up to the bank, tied the boat off, got out my chair I had on the boat, and set beside Sam. I told 'er, "I shore wish y'all had seen the weddin'. It shore were nice, and Sarah were a purty girl, jist like y'all. They got a ranch there. Bill's gonna run it. John's in love with Carla, but 'er mama wants 'er to finish school first afore they git married. Can't blame 'er. Bill give John all them boats and everythin' he had here. I'm shore John can run them boats. Well, Sam, I love y'all. It's not much fun to live without y'all here."

I put the chair back in the boat and sed, "I love y'all, Sam. I'll be back."

I started the boat and headed back to Homosassa. The sunset on the water shore looked purty. I landed the boat, tied it up, and John walked up. He sed, "Did y'all tell 'er 'bout the weddin'?"

I sed, "Yes, I did. I'll be glad when I'm with 'er."

Trip to Bill's

Chapter 32

Several years later, I called Bill on Sally's phone. Sarah answered it. I asked if'n Bill were there. She sed, "He's in the barn with the boys."

I told 'er I thought I'd come visit for a while. She sed, "Come on. Be glad to see y'all."

I left in my truck. It's gotten old, and rust from livin' on the Gulf 'bout et it up, but it still runs good. I left 'bout 8 that mornin'. It were mistin' rain, but it weren't cold. Jist a nice day. I began thinkin' 'bout when we left Center Hill in the wagon. It took us a long time to come from Inverness to Homosassa, which ain't that far in a car. That wagon were slow, and Pete and Kate was slow, but they would walk all day. I 'membered when Pete died. Ole Kate jist stood there and looked at 'im. It weren't long till she died, too. Them was real good mules.

I were comin' in to Inverness. That town shore has growed lots. They say they's a man in Inverness makes the best buggies in the United States. I bought one, one time, and I'd still go in it, but I don't use horses no more.

I had 'bout 3 miles to go to git to Bill's ranch. I seen a man standin' on the side of the road. I stopped to give 'im a ride. I asked where he were goin'. He sed, "I'm lookin' for a job."

I sed, "What kind of work do y'all do?"

He sed, "I don't have no education, but jist know how to do hard work. But if'n I had 5 dollars, I think I'd go back to Georgia."

I sed, "Is that what a bus ticket costs?"

He sed, "Yes."

So I turned the truck 'round and headed to the bus station. I bought 'im a ticket to Georgia. Then I give 'im 3 dollars to git 'im somethin' to eat.

He thanked me and I went back toward Bill's. It were 'bout 10 when I got there. I stopped at the house. It shore were a nice house. They were a big porch all the way 'round the house. I knocked on the door and Sarah come to the door.

I seen by the bump on 'er stomach that they was gonna have another baby. She sed, "Bill's in the barn."

So I went to the barn to find 'im. Bill were busy cleanin' the barn and hangin' what done fell down. He looked up and sed, "Dad, I shore am glad to see y'all. I've been so busy I jist couldn't leave the ranch."

I sed, "Where's the boys?"

He jist laughed. "They's in the cow pen fightin' in all that cow poop. They do it all the time. They git mad at each other, but in the cow poop they's an even match, so I let 'em fight it out. They know what their mama's gonna do to 'em when they come home with cow poop all over 'em though."

Bill called the boys. They come runnin' for me. I yelled, "No!"

But Bill stopped 'em afore they got to me. He told 'em to come over by the hose and he hosed 'em off. Then he made 'em take off their clothes and handed 'em some soap to wash. They cleaned up purty good.

Bill sent 'em to the house to git some clean, dry clothes, but instead, they put on their wet clothes. We still sent 'em to the house. Bill laughed and sed, "Their mama will whip both of 'em. They do this all the time, and we laugh 'bout it every night. I don't care where I go, they jist wanna go to be with me."

I sed, "I like that."

He sed, "Let me hitch up the buggy and I'll take y'all to see the ranch." It would take 3-4 days to see it all.

We looked up and here come the boys. He told one of the boys to git the rifle. He sed, "We may see a snake." They done kill a bunch of 'em already. The swamp were full of 'em.

The oldest boy, Kyle, run inside and got the rifle and a box of bullets. He handed the gun to Bill and both boys climbed in. Bill put it by the seat. We went down the road 'bout a mile and stopped at an ole house with a barn out back. I looked at it and knowed I'd been there afore. Then Bill sed, "I think this is the place where Lewis and y'all kilt 2 bears. The people that own it sold it to Sarah's mom and dad."

I sed, "Can I see the barn?"

He sed, "Shore."

I walked in the barn, and then I knowed it were the place where Lewis and I kilt 2 deer with jist one shot, too. "The man that owns this place tried to give my dad a homestead, but he sed, 'No, we was goin' fishin.'"

I felt like I jist wanted to cry. This coulda been home for us.

When we got back in the buggy we rode through the swamp. Nick, the youngest son sed, "There's a snake."

He put one bullet in his dad's gun. I seen the boy lookin' for the best shot, then he fired. The head of that rattlesnake flew off.

He sed, "They's another one somewhere close by."

We looked, but didn't find one. Then he wanted the rattle off 'im. Bill let 'im get 'em sometimes, but even if'n he were dead he'd strike again. So he got a stick and held 'is head away from 'im to cut off the rattle. Then he wanted the skin, but Bill told 'im, "No. They stink too bad."

Bill told me, "Them boys has every kind of skin y'all could think of.

I asked Bill, "Do y'all miss the boat and the river?"

He sed, "Every once in a while I do, but I love this so much. My wife and boys would like it, but I think the boys love this.

We traveled through the swamp, then through the open field of beautiful grass. I looked 'round. They was cows everywhere, and they were a big ole bull. The grass were high. Bill sed, "I'm gonna cut hay tomorrow. A crew's comin' in."

I sed, "How many cows do y'all have now?"

He sed, "I don't really know, but we have lots of land. It's in the thousands, I'm thinkin'. I got 3 ranch foremen, and they take care of most of it.

He sed, "I got somethin' I want to talk to you 'bout. Did y'all know John's sellin' the boats, and he bought 400 acreas in Dade City? It's all cleared and has a good fence. They's a nice house on the land. Even though I owned part of the boat, I don't want nothin' out of it."

I sed, "I knowed he be marryin' Carla afore long."

He sed, "He shore is."

He laughed and sed, "I bet them 2 will have a red-headed boy, and he'll jist do 'em in. Y'all tell John to 'member that I gave 'im everythin' that I own in them boats for an early weddin' gift. I 'member y'all tellin' me what that mullet fisherman told y'all. 'Never be greedy.' I think 'is name were Ray. He musta been a good man."

I sed, "He were."

Bill sed, "You tell John if'n I don't get invited to the weddin' he'll have to work at my ranch. No, jist kiddin'. Tell John I'm gonna give 'im some fine cows and a good bull too. That'll give 'im somethin' to work with. I have more money than I could ever spend. We can have any-thin' we want from Sarah's dad. And Sarah and I have a love like y'all and Mama had. So if'n y'all want, I'll build a house where the barn is. Y'all can eat y'all's meals with us. I'll send the boys over to pick y'all up every day."

I looked at Bill with tears in my eyes and sed, "I jist can't leave Sam at the river. I hope to stay there till I die. I don't think it will be much longer. I done got old."

Bill sed, "Well, y'all are gonna spend the night here, ain't y'all?"

But I sed, "No. I'm gonna go back home."

But Sarah wanted me to stay. She done fix steak, beans, collard greens that she growed in 'er garden and made an apple pie. She sed, "Y'all gotta stay."

So I sed, "Well, guess I can."

"The boys already asked if'n they can sleep with y'all, but I sed they couldn't. They jist think so much of y'all. Do you ever hear from Lewis' girls?"

I sed, "Ever once in a while. I hear that they's busy cleanin' fish, and they smell like fish, but they's rich. They told me they's even gonna retire soon."

We went inside. Sarah had the table set. "Y'all set there in that chair, or I'll have a fight on my hands. Them boys wanna set on each side of y'all." I jist laughed.

We et supper. I noticed they got 2 boxes for the boys to stand on to wash the dishes. I loved what I seen.

Bill looked at me and sed, "They wash the dishes every night. And they git paid. So, when they's 18, they'll have 10,000 dollars in the bank. That's for a new car."

When they was through with the dishes they come out and set with me. They asked me about catchin' the crooks, and were I scared.

I looked at 'em and sed, "Yes, I were. I were only 16 years old, and I thought they'd kill me, but I hada do it."

The other boy sed, "Were it fun?"

I sed, "No, and I hope y'all never have to do nothin' like it."

Sarah came in and told the boys to go take their bath. They sed, "We done had a bath."

But Bill sed, "Well, take another one." And they done it.

We set on the screen porch and listened to the frogs and all the night critters. They was some noises we didn't know what they was. Sarah brought us a cup of coffee. The air were a little cool, but it felt good.

Sarah put the boys to bed in the same bed and told me I could sleep in the other one. Then she sed, "Why don't y'all come and live with us? The boys shore would like that."

I sed, "I jist can't leave Sam. I'd have to have her moved here. Did Bill tell y'all where she is?"

She sed, "Yes, he did. And I don't see nothin' wrong with that. That's where y'all want to go, too, ain't it?"

I sed, "Yes, it are."

She sed, "Love's a funny thang. I would hate to know that Bill wouldn't be comin' home every night.

I sed, "I'm tired. Think I'll take a shower and go to bed."

I took my shower and started to git in bed, but I looked at the boys and moved 'em to one side. I slipped in bed with 'em. I laid there jist a few minutes, and I were sound asleep.

Next mornin' the boys was shakin' me to come et breakfast. So I got up, put my clothes and shoes on, combed my hair, and washed my face.

I walked in to the dinin' room. It were a big breakfast. We et and then Sarah sed, "Boys, I'll do the dishes this mornin'. Y'all can have a rest, jist this one time."

I hugged Sarah and told Bill and the boys, "Goodbye".

Bill sed, "Go by the Ford place and git y'all a new truck. I'll pay for it."

I jist looked at 'im. I left 'bout 9 and drove back to Inverness. I stopped at the Ford place. The salesman come out and sed my truck don't look so good. It were et up with rust. Well, I weren't gonna trade it in, and it weren't none of 'is business if'n it were bad. Then I told 'im that I were comin' to buy a new truck, but I wanted it now.

Another man come outside, stopped me and sed, "He's jist a little of a hot head. I'd like to show y'all a new truck."

The new trucks shore done looked nice. I seen a green truck I liked and sed, "How much are y'all askin' for that one?"

He sed, "Y'all want to trade y'all's old one in?"

I sed, "No. I'll give it to the boy at the river."

The price weren't too bad, but I told 'im that my son bought 6 trucks there last month and sed, "If'n y'all don't give me a good deal, I'll buy the next one in Tampa."

He asked who my son were, and I told 'im, "Bill Fussell." He looked at me real funny and then knocked off 500 dollars more.

I asked, "Will y'all take my check?"

He sed, "What's y'all's name?"

I sed, "Red Fussell."

He looked at me and sed, "I sold y'all a Model T with a girl under a blanket."

I sed, "That's right. She died 'bout 4 years ago."

I wrote 'im a check and he asked, "Is y'all's old truck runnin' good?"

I sed, "It shore is."

He sed, "Let me show y'all somethin' I have out back."

He walked to the back, and there were a good-lookin' pickup. He sed, "It needs a new motor, but if'n your truck has a good motor, we'll sell y'all the truck cheap and put y'all's motor in it for 500 dollars, and we'll keep the rest of the rusty truck."

I sed, "Let's do it, but y'all will need to bring it to Homosassa."

He sed, "I can do that."

So I paid 'im. I left in the new truck. Whew Doggie! It shore did drive good. It even had a radio, and it smelled good. I thought, *I shore ain't gonna haul none of Lewis' girls for while. They smell like fish.* And I jist laughed out loud.

I got home and called Bill, but Sarah answered the phone. I sed, "I had a real good time at y'all's house. Tell Bill I done bought a new truck on my way home."

She sed, "The boys shore loved y'all's visit too. And when they found y'all asleep with 'em they was real excited."

They brought the truck that I had the motor put in. I give it to Sally's daughter, Jill. She were 'bout 16. She hugged me and told me she loved me. That jist warmed my ole heart.

Trip to Tampa

Chapter 33

The trip to Tampa warn't very long. I stopped by the fish camp and walked inside. They was all cleanin' fish. They had a big ole freezer. They shipped the fish in 50-pound pasteboard boxes. The train pulled in, and they shipped a boxcar-load a day.

Lewis told me he were gonna quit next week and give 'is girls the business. He sed, "They run it anyway." He told me he had all the money he needed and thought he'd move back to Okahumpka. Maybe he'd buy a small farm where he could grow jist what he wanted. His wife was tired of fish. He told me that if'n I wanted to, I could go with 'em.

But I told 'im I didn't wanna move. I loved the Gulf.

Sam's sister, Judy, lived in Okahumpka on Clearwater Lake. They own an orange grove and a bunch of kids, 4 or 5. They's a carload. Lewis thought I might know where they's a farm with good land. So I sed, "Why don't we go right now and look?"

Lewis sed he wanted to talk to 'is wife first, that she might wanna go along. And she did. So Lewis sed, "Why don't y'all take y'all's truck back home, and we'll pick y'all up tomorrow. "

They showed up 'bout 8:30 the next mornin'. The weather were nice with a light wind and not hot. We et a bite at Sally's. She always has a good meal. I told Lewis to stop at Sandy's to tell 'er where we was goin'. I knowed that red-headed boy of mine would be down there. I told

Sandy we was headed to Okahumpka to look at some land. She sed she'd tell John.

I told Lewis to pull 'is car down by the dock and I'd fill it with gas. And we checked the oil. We drove through Inverness, then down some dirt roads. I sed, "Stop, Lewis." He stopped and asked what were wrong. I sed, "See that big oak there. We camped there when we left Center Hill, and jist down the road is where we shot them men."

He sed, "It shore is. That were a long time ago. Them was hard times, and we slept in the hay. Do y'all 'member when we shot them 3 robbers?"

I sed, "I shore do."

We drove on down the road to the Withlacoochee River where we crossed back then. Now there's a bridge there. It cost 50 cents to cross back then, but I told Lewis that 'is father-in-law paid for it. We didn't know it then, but he were rich. That's what he bought the fish camp with, and it's been a money maker ever since.

I told 'im, " 'Member what y'all sed about y'all's future wife?"

Lewis sed, "No. What'd I say?"

I told 'im, "Y'all sed, 'She shore were purty.'"

Lewis laughed and sed, "She still are."

We rode on through to Center Hill, but didn't stop there. We got to Okahumpka to Judy's house. They was a hog in their yard, chickens on the porch, and 2 or 3 dogs in the yard. She come out of the house and were real glad to see us. She sed, "Come on in."

I looked at Lewis. He weren't shore he wanted to. I knowed he thought that house would be a mess, but it were as clean as it could be. Her husband, Jack, sed he knowed where there were a nice farm for 300 dollars, with a house that needed to be fixed up, 'bout 3 miles down the road.

So we went to check it out. We turned on a sand road and drove up to that house. It did need a lot of work. I told Lewis that if'n it were me, I'd build a new house, and that right there where they stood, were 'bout 12 acres. "Do you like it, Lewis?"

He sed, "Yes, I do."

I took my money pouch out and handed the man 300 dollars. "It's y'all's, Lewis." I told 'im, "I always wanted to do that."

I told the man to send the deed to Lewis Fussell, Box 4962, Tampa,

The Mullet Boys

FL. And I asked 'im to burn the other house down. But the man sed he'd like to have the wood from the house. He'd git 'is boys to do it this week.

I didn't want Lewis to know I were gonna build it for 'im so I had to talk to Judy alone. I asked 'er who could build a house, and told 'er we'd be back in a week.

We left Okahumpka and went back to Tampa to look at house plans. He picked out what he wanted, and told me he'd pick the plans up some day. Well, I picked 'em up and put 'em in my suit case. Lewis took me home. I were glad to be back home.

The next day I left for Okahumpka again. I stopped at Jack and Judy's house and asked if'n she found a builder. She sed 'er boys could build it. That's what they done for a livin'.

So I called 'em. She had a phone. She called 3 of 'er sons to come over. They looked at the plans and sed they could build it with no problem. So I asked, "How much would it cost me?"

They sed, "Let us look at the plans in detail and give 'em to the lumber yard. They can tell us how much it would cost."

I stayed at Jack and Judy's house for 3 days. I seen the orange groves and cow pasture. I asked 'im, "Don't y'all's boys like cows?"

Jack sed, "No, they don't. I have one boy that works with me, and the other likes to build houses. They's good at what they do."

The boys come out to tell me what it would cost, and told me it would be a real nice house. I told 'em that it would be painted inside and out. But they jist laughed and sed, "It will be brick on the outside and painted on the inside, and the electric will be installed. Some day Lewis can git the electricity hooked up. The price would be 7 thousand dollars, and it'll take us 'bout 5 months to finish it, but the lumber company wants some money now."

I asked, "How much money do they need now?"

He didn't know, and sed, "We gotta go find out."

So we went to lumber company and asked how much they needed down now.

They sed, "Well, 5 thousand should do it."

I asked at the lumber company if'n these boys was good builders. The man said, "Them are the best builders. If'n I were gonna build a house, I'd want 'em to do it."

I got my money bag out and counted out what they wanted.

He sed, "I'll write y'all a receipt for the money."

I sed, "I don't need no receipt."

But he sed, "Y'all need one." And he wrote it.

I went to where Lewis' land were. They had it all cleaned up. I asked where the well were, and they showed it to me. I sed, 'Is it good water?"

And they sed, "Yes, real good water." I went back to the house and told 'em I needed to pay the boys.

But Judy sed, "Jist give me the money and I'll pay 'em."

The boys drove up and walked in. I sed, "When do you start workin' on the house? Your mother sed to pay 'er for the well, and she'd pay y'all."

One boy sed, "She probably won't pay us all the money." And he laughed.

I asked, "How much money do y'all want now to start to build?"

They sed, "600 dollars now, and when we get the roof on, the rest would be 2,000 dollars for labor. Is that alright?"

I told 'em it were. I handed 'em 600 dollars and they split it up.

I waited 'bout 3 months, and then come to check on the house. When I drove down the road I stopped dead in my tracks. There were one of the best lookin' houses I ever seen. It had brick on the sides and a big ole fireplace. I walked inside. It had wood panelin'. I shore did like that, and it had good lookin' windows, strong wood doors and the kitchen had runnin' water, but I didn't know how they done that. Then I seen the windmill pumpin' water, and in the middle were an electric motor turnin' the windmill. They had a big water tank and a big wood stove. They wasn't no wood yet, but I shore liked what I seen. I shore hope Lewis likes it.

The boys got there and told me they would be done in a week. So I give 'em the rest of the money I owed 'em, and I left to go back to Homosassa.

I called Lewis and told 'im I were goin' to Okahumpka, and asked if'n he'd like to go with me. He did. So I told Lewis I'd come by and git 'im.

I asked John if'n I could borrow 'is car, and he sed, "Shore." So I stopped to pick Lewis and 'is wife up. We made it to Okahumpka in 'bout 2 hours. When we drove down that dirt road, he seen that house there on 'is land. He couldn't believe 'is eyes. They got out of the car and walked up to the house to look inside. Everythin' were done!

He looked at me and sed, "Why did y'all do this?"

I sed, "Y'all never got nothin' out of y'all's share. That man taught me how to fish, and he told me to never be greedy. That money paid for it all." They looked it all over and he shore did like it.

I told 'im, "I need to go to the lumber company to see if'n they had enough money."

At the lumber company they told me I had 600 dollars comin' back to me. I told 'em to give it to them boys that built the house.

As we started back to Tampa, Lewis sed, "Red, I need to tell y'all. I've been real sick. I don't know how much longer I'll live."

I sed, "Well, the house is y'all's. If'n y'all want to, y'all can sell it and it will be fine with me."

He sed, "I jist might do that." Then I asked 'im, "Do y'all need money?"

He sed, "No, but I think I need to stay in Tampa."

So I told 'im to sell the new house. I understood. Lewis were hopin' it didn't upset me, but I assured 'im, I weren't upset and that I jist liked doin' it. He told me that he'd git my money back to me, but I jist laughed and told 'im, "Ain't my house. It's what y'all had comin', and y'all never done git y'all's part."

I let 'em out and went back to Homosassa. I heard later that Lewis sold the house. I didn't ask what he got for it, but somebody done got a nice house.

John's Weddin'

Chapter 34

I were down at the dock and seen John come up. He walked to the dock and set down. He sed, "Dad, I done sold all the boats. I got the church painted, and I'm movin' to Dade City. That's where Carla and I is gonna live. I know I'll miss them boats, but that's what I wanna do."

I sed, "Then that's what I want y'all to do. I talked to Bill 'bout 'is part of the boats."

John sed, "'Member, Bill told me they's a weddin' gift? He don't want nothin'." John went on to say, "Come live with us. Y'all can help on the ranch. I'd like to pay for y'all's new truck. You know, y'all made us rich. I'll always have to work, but I don't mind workin'. I jist don't wanna be gone out fishin' for a week at a time. I 'member when y'all was gone, Mama worried all the time. Storms, bad people, or jist bad luck."

I sed, "I want y'all to be happy."

John sed, "Next week Carla and me, we're gonna have the weddin'."

I sed, "You'd better let that Fussell bunch know 'bout it."

He sed, "We done sent everybody a card. I shore hope they show up. We're goin' to Dade City right after the weddin'. I bought 400 acre-as, then the thousand acreas next to it. That thousand has to be cleared. And I bought some heavy equipment to do the work. Carla's gonna help me. It'll be fun. Come help us."

I sed, "Y'all know I can't leave this here river."

He sed, "Love shore is a funny thang. I love Carla, jist like y'all loved Mama."

The week passed real quick. Sally made the weddin' cake. It shore looked nice. The day of the weddin' Judy and her bunch showed up. Whew Doggie! They coulda filled a Greyhound bus, but they's a good bunch. They got a real good ranch.

I were settin' on the dock and seen Bill drive in. Out jumped the 2 boys of 'is. I still can't keep their names straight. One is Kyle and the other is Nick, but I get 'em mixed up. They run to the dock and give me a hug. It made me feel real good.

Then Bill told them to stay off the dock. I knowed what that were for. He were 'fraid they'd fall off it, or one would push the other off into the water.

He sed, "Sarah don't feel so good."

Sed, "Sorry to hear that."

Bill sed, "I love them cows."

I sed, "John now has 1,400 acreas for 'is ranch, but they have to clear most of it."

I looked up and here come John. He turned and went in my house. Then he come back out and walked up to Bill. He sed, "Bill, I feel bad 'bout takin' all the money on our boats. Let's split it; here's y'all's part of the boats."

Bill looked at it and sed, "Y'all forgot to sign the check." And he handed it back to John.

I didn't know what were goin' on. Then John looked where y'all sign it, and Bill done tore that part off. John looked at Bill and sed, "I'll give y'all all of it if'n y'all want it. Y'all's been real good to me."

Bill sed, "Let's have a race, jist like we done when we was kids."

John laughed and sed, "Not with y'all. Y'all always win."

Then Bill sed, "Y'all take it for y'all's weddin' gift, and I'm givin' y'all 40 good cows and 2 bulls too. I'll deliver 'em 2 weeks after the weddin'. I want y'all to have it."

John thanked 'im and sed, "I gotta go git ready for my weddin'."

Bill sed, "Ole Ray were right – never be greedy. It brings y'all a lot of happiness."

Afore long, Lewis' girls drove up, and Bill sed, "I bet they smell like fish." They helped their mama out of the car. They all shore looked nice. The cars jist kept comin'.

I were standin' outside the church when a man come up to me. I knowed 'im but jist couldn't place 'im. Then I 'membered. It were the policeman from down the road. He shore looked bad. I sed, "Good to see y'all. Are y'all still a policeman down the the road?"

He sed, "No. They won't let me work no more. Them bank robbers shot me when I stopped 'em. They shot me up purty good. So I can't work no more."

Sed, "Well, I'm shore glad y'all made it to the weddin'." He nodded and walked off. I didn't know what to say.

Then here come Clem. Whew Doggie! He cleans up real good. Them girls and Sandy looked like roses jist openin'. Carla loves my red-headed boy jist like I do. They's so much in love.

They took Clem's family to their seat. Clem had to give 'is daughter away. I told Bill to set up front with me and to bring Kyle and Nick with 'im.

There stood John with the preacher. He were shakin'. I thought it were funny. That's what I did when I got married, and I wanted to laugh. They started to play the piano. Carla walked in and I seen that boy of mine. His heart were 'bout to blow up.

Then Clem brought 'er up front. I don't know what he sed, but all I could think of were Sam. I wish she were here. At times I even wish I coulda died so she could live, but I don't want it that way neither.

The weddin' were over and they started out the door. Everyone were throwin' rice at 'em. Them kids done put tin cans on the back of John's car. John opened the door, Carla got in and they drove away.

When they left, I walked over to Clem and Sandy. Sandy had tears in 'er eyes. She sed, "I'm so happy for Carla, I don't know what to do."

I told them I'd buy supper for them and the girls, and they sed, "Okay."

I borrowed Judy's car. We all got in and drove to Inverness to a fancy restaurant. I'd jist as soon et at Sally's, but them young girls needed somethin' to do. When we stopped I told the girls, "Y'all can have whatever y'all want. Don't look at the prices. Jist look at what y'all want."

As we walked in the door they were a man there. I knowed 'im, but couldn't place 'im. I spoke and he spoke back. We et our meal and I asked for the bill. But the server sed the bill had done been paid.

I seen that man at the door and stopped and thanked 'im for payin' and sed, "I know y'all, but jist can't place y'all."

He sed, "I needed help real bad one time, and y'all give me all the money y'all had on y'all. I done well, and I've always looked for a way to pay y'all back."

I sed, "I didn't give it to y'all for y'all to pay it back, but I thank y'all."

He left. I didn't 'member givin' 'im no money, but I may have. I asked the girls if'n they'd like some ice cream.

Clem spoke up real fast and sed, "Yes." We all laughed. We got some ice cream and then drove back to Homosassa. I thanked Judy for the use of 'er car, and she jist laughed.

'Bout 3 weeks later I asked Sandy if'n the girls could go to Dade City to see Carla and John. She sed, "Can I go too?"

I sed, "Shore." So we all crowded in my truck and rode over to John's place. I hadn't been on 'is ranch afore, but shore liked what I seen. We drove up to the gate and blowed the horn, 2 short and 1 long. I seen a big truck comin' 'cross the pasture.

Out stepped Carla. Her mama likeda flipped. Carla had on pants!!! They was dirty and so were 'er hair. Her mama sed, "What have y'all been doin'?"

Carla sed, "It's hard work, but some day we'll have a big ranch. I'm clearin' land. Let me call John."

She went over to the pump and pulled a cord. A whistle blowed 2 short and 1 long. In jist a few minutes John were there. Carla sed, "Let me clean up a bit. John, take y'all's dad to show 'im the ranch."The girls went to the house with Carla.

I got in an ole truck. They warn't even no doors, but it run good. John sed. "It come with the house."

So we rode over to where they was clearin' land. I asked John, "What were Carla drivin' out there?"

He pointed to a big ole tractor with a rake on the front. "She were pushin' up stumps."

I sed, "Did y'all teach 'er?"

He sed, "No, she jist got on it and made a mess. Then she got better and better. Now she does a real good job. Come on, I want to show y'all an ole house on the thousand acreas."

'Bout half a mile down the road we come to a bunch a trees. I sed, "I've been here afore."

He sed, "Are y'all shore?"

I sed, "Yes. I'm shore."

We rode on up to the house. I looked, and I knowed I'd been here and sed, "This is where I kilt 'em 2 men that kilt my dad. I laid over there in that bunch of trees for 'bout 2 weeks. It rained and it were cold. I et dried fish and the root of palmetto and drunk rain water. My insides jist shook. I still 'member what it looked like when them men fell. I can rest now. I were 'bout a 16 years old then, but knowed it hada be did. It were still bad."

We rode up to the house. It shore were run down. Then John sed, "Want me to burn it down?"

I sed, "Not really. It's jist an ole house."

Then John sed, "I'll let Carla push it over and burn it."

We left and rode over to the spring. It were a big spring. They would always be water for the cows. We went back to the house. Carla cleaned up and John sed, "I need a bath."

They had a windmill that pumped water in a big tank, and they had a generator that made electricity to charge the battery. She cooked on a gas stove and she had a wood stove, too. John sed, "When she cooks on that wood stove, we cut wood all day."

I jist laughed. "Them wood stoves shore burn a lot of wood, so somebody has to cut it."

Carla were cookin' some up the frog legs they gigged the night afore. Her sister were makin' biskits and helpin' 'er fix the meal. It shore were good when they finished. They didn't have no ice, but we had tea anyway. We et and the girls cleaned it all up.

We set on the porch and looked out at the pasture. Then John sed, "There's cows in that pasture. Bill put 'em there."

He went on to say, "Bill shore has been good to me and Carla. He knows a lot more 'bout cows than I do. When I go to buy more cows, I'll ask 'im to help me buy a good brand of cows."

I asked, "What brand y'all gonna use?"

He sed, "I think I'll use what Bill think's I should."

I finally sed, "I wanna get back afore dark." So Carla hugged 'er mama and both of 'er sisters and told 'em she wanted them to come and stay this summer when school were out. They agreed. Sandy could tell the girls was gonna leave some day, and it made 'er sad. She didn't cry, but she still may.

We went back to Homosassa and got there afore dark. I looked at the dock and knowed right away somethin' were wrong. The girls thanked me; they had a good time and they went in the house.

I walked down to the dock. The lawman were there, so I asked 'im what were wrong, but he told me to leave.

I walked back to Sam's sister and asked 'er if'n she knowed what were wrong. She sed, "At the dock, one of the workers kilt the man that owns the boat."

They'd have to go to court in Tampa, somethin' to do with the Gulf.

I went back down to the dock to see how it happened. I asked one of 'is boys what happened and he told me, "It ain't none of y'all's business."

Well, that made me mad. I didn't say nothin'. I jist went over to the bench and set down.

The law done left, but the boys was still there. One come up and sed, "Why don't y'all go home? Keep y'all's nose out of our business."

I really got mad then. I let them park their boat at my dock and didn't charge 'em nothin'. I got up and walked to the boat. The boy walked out and started to say somethin' but I sed, "First, git y'all's boat away from my dock, and y'all can git y'all's ice somewhere else."

He told me, "I'll move when I'm good and ready."

Well, I were gittin' madder by the minute. I went up to Sally's, shut off the electricity and water and told 'er not to sell 'em any ice.

She sed, "I ain't never seen y'all this mad!"

I seen them come on the deck of the boat. Now they was mad. They told me, "If'n you don't turn it back on, we'll call the sheriff."

I sed, "Good. Go ahead."

They did. The sheriff come and wanted to know why I shut the electricity and water off. And then he told me, "They done had a bad day. They's dad were the one that got kilt. He were beatin' the man that shot 'im. So I turned the man loose. He were jist protectin' himself. The boys told me their dad were bad sometimes, even to them."

I thought 'bout it, and turned the water and electricity back on. Then I walked down to the dock and told 'em I were sorry for the way I

James Carlton Fussell

acted, and sorry their dad got kilt.

They sed, "We'll move the boat in a day or two."

But I sed, "Y'all don't gotta do that."

Cow Thieves

Chapter 35

I ain't been to John and Carla's in 'bout 6 months. I did go to see Bill, but he were busy, so I didn't stay long.

Back in Homosassa, I looked up from the dock and here come John's truck in a hurry.

He sed, "Dad, let's go see Bill."

I sed, "Well, let me go tell Sally I'll be gone."

I got in the truck. I never seen 'im drive so fast. Finally he sed, "Somebody stole 5 of my cows last night. I called the law, but they don't know what to do."

After several minutes, John sed, "By the way, I were so upset over my missing cows I forgot to tell you. We jist found out, we're gonna have a baby."

I sed, "Well, congratulations."

We got to Bill's and John knocked on the door. Sarah opened the door. John sed, "Where's Bill?"

She sed, "He's over at Swamp Ranch in the long pasture."

Well, John didn't know where the long pasture were, but Nick sed, "I know where it are. I can take y'all over there."

They had a new little baby named Steve. He looked jist like Sarah. Afore we left to go find Bill, we looked up and here come Kyle with the baby in 'is arms.

Sarah sed, "He shore do love that baby."

Then Nick hitched up the buggy to ride over to Swamp Ranch in long pasture. He done a good job. Then he got the rifle and a box of bullets. It were a 30-30 rifle. John thought he'd git the 22 rifle, but this one's alright. It shore felt good with 'im drivin' the buggy. You could tell he done this all the time.

We all 3 rode through the swamp. I looked over to the right and I quietly sed, "Stop. Don't say nothin'. Jist back up there." The tree line hid us. They was a truck loadin' up cows. I sed, "Nick, is that y'all's dad out there?"

He sed, "No. He's gotta black truck. It ain't like that one."

John picked up the rifle and the box of bullets. Then he told me to take Nick and go back to the house and call the sheriff. I told Nick to not leave in a hurry and not to make no noise till we got out of sight.

Nick sed, "I'll jist stay with y'all, Uncle John."

But he sed, "No, I need y'all to go with Grandpa."

John crawled in the palmetto patch. He could see real good from here. He layed there 'bout 30 minutes. As close as he could tell they was 5 of 'em, maybe 6. The odds was not good. But surprise may save 'im. He could hear talkin', but when he heard 'em say, "That's 'bout all we can haul." He knowed he'd have to make 'is move.

They was 3 of 'em thieves standin' close at the back of the trailer, and he could see someone on the other side of the trailer. He thought, *I gotta make my move now.* So he raised up and clicked. He done forgot to put the shells in the rifle! So he real quick-like put in 6 shells. He shore were glad he didn't run at 'em.

They done moved 'round some. Then 4 of 'em was standin' close together. So he could shoot the hats off their heads. He got in a good position then, and shot 4 times and 4 hats flew off. He hollered, "Git next to the trailer with y'all's hands on the trailer."

One man reached for 'is gun, and John shot and knicked 'is ear. Then he hollered, "Hey! Don't kill me!"

So John sed, "Then do what I say."

John knowed they was 2 more, maybe 3. One made a run for the woods and then he run back with 'is hands up and put 'em on the trailer. John didn't know what happened and why he come back.

Then another one run and he hollered. He fired 5-6 times, and

The Mullet Boys

then he come back out with 'is hands up. John still didn't know what happened.

John told 'em to tell that other feller to come out. He fired a round in John's direction, so John moved. He climbed a big ole oak tree so he could see 'em better. He could see 'im, but couldn't git a good shot. He didn't wanna kill 'im.

John could see 'im slippin' in the tree line. Then he heard 'im shoot 5-6 times, but not at 'im. John still wondered what the man were shootin' at. John got the shot he needed. He shot 'is gun in 'is hand. When the bullet hit the gun it scared 'im. He dropped it down and put 'is hands up.

John didn't move. He could hear someone comin'. There I were with Bill, the sheriff and a bunch of help. I walked up to the men with their hands up, and looked at one of the men. I knowed who he were. He were the kid I let go when I shot 'is dad, but he'd been there when they killed my dad.

Bill walked up. He looked in the trailer. Shore 'nuff, they was 'is cows. He asked who were in charge, but nobody sed a word. I seen one man who looked real scared. John walked out of the woods.

I told Bill to get somethin' to dig a hole. He looked at me real funny. I sed, "Jist git it."

They had a loader close by. I told the sheriff what I were gonna do to catch all 'em cow thieves. He sed, "Do it."

The sheriff left with 'em crooks, except the one that looked so scared, but they didn't go far. I looked at the scared one. I told Bill to dig me a deep hole.

The man that were standin' there sed, "What y'all gonna do to me?"

I sed, "We hang cow thieves, and I'll bury y'all in that hole. They won't never find y'all. Y'all got a wife and kids?"

He sed, "Yes. Please don't kill me."

I sed, "Get me a rope."

The man started to cry. So I sed, "Tell me where y'all're takin' the cows."

He sed, "They'll kill me if'n I tell y'all."

So I sed, "And I'll kill y'all if'n y'all don't."

I told Bill to get the sheriff back. He road up and asked, "What's up?"

James Carlton Fussell

I sed, "This here man's gonna tell us where they take the cows. I told 'im y'all'd set 'im free if'n he told the truth. If'n he lies, I'll take care of 'im."

The sheriff sed, "Is that so? How do I know y'all are tellin' the truth."

I sed, "My name's Red Fussell. Ask anybody. If'n I give my word, it's so."

I turned to the man and sed, "Now, where do y'all take the cows?"

He sed, "'Bout 2 miles south of Lake City. But I want to tell y'all, that sheriff down there's in on the cow stealin' in Lake City."

I sed, "Where do they take 'em?"

He sed, "To Jacksonville, to the meat packin' plant."

Bill and John were listenin' to all this and sed, "Let's go to Lake City."

We come to the house to tell Sarah where we was goin'. We dressed the part in ole clothes and ole hats, with side arms and drove behind the truck.

We got to Lake City 'bout 6 in the mornin'. When we pulled in to the lot; the sheriff were there. They was 'bout 10 people. The sheriff sed, "How many y'all got?"

I sed, "10 head nice cows. I'd sure like to git paid so I can leave."

He sed, "How much?"

I sed, "20 a head."

The sheriff sed, "That ain't a bad price." And he handed me the money.

I pulled my pistol and put it on the sheriff's nose. I sed, "If'n you move I'll pull the trigger."

The other feller started to run, but it were too late. They was all arrested. They loaded 'em up and took 'em back to Inverness.

We waited in Lake City till they got back. The Inverness sheriff were laughin'. He sed, "That stealin' sheriff tried everythin' to keep from goin' to jail. He even sed he'd give state's evidence if'n we turn 'im loose."

We left Lake City 'bout midnight and backed in the loadin' ramp in Jacksonville. The night foreman come out.

Bill and John and I walked out on the loadin' ramp. I sed, "Are y'all the one I do business with?"

He looked at me and sed, "Are them cows stolen?"

I sed, "Yes. We got 'em 2 nights ago. Do y'all care if'n they's stolen?"

The Mullet Boys

He sed, "No, stolen cows eat jist as good."

I sed, "What do y'all pay a head?"

He sed, "Let me look at 'em." He looked and sed, "30 dollars."

I sed, "That's cheap."

He sed, "That's all I give for stolen cows."

I sed, "I'll take it."

He paid us cash and he started to walk away. I stuck my gun in 'is back and here come the Inverness sheriff right behind me. They hauled 'im off to jail and then they shut the place down.

'Afore they was done, they done caught all 3 of 'is sons, too.

Lewis

Chapter 36

The mailman come by and sed Lewis died last night. They was gonna bury 'im on Friday. He'd been sick a long time. I told Sally I needed a box of smoked mullet to take with me. Thursday I got ready to go in my pickup truck to Tampa to see if'n I could do anythin'.

But first, I stopped and picked up the mullet to put in the truck. Then I stopped at Clem and Sandy's. I told Sandy that if'n anyone should need anythin' afore I got home, I would pay for it when I got back.

On the way to Tampa, I seen that policeman that were raised in Homosassa. I stopped, and he told me 'is dad died 'bout a year ago. I told 'im that my brother jist died and I was on the way to Tampa to see what I could do. He asked, "Do you ever git over a death?"

I sed, "No."

I told 'im to come and see us sometime.

In 'bout an hour I were in Tampa. I drove to the fish camp. They was packin' all the fish they had, and told them fishermen not to bring no more fish till Tuesday.

They sed that Lewis went to sleep one night and jist didn't wake up. I guess that's the best way to go, but there ain't no good way.

I'll still miss 'im. His daughters hugged my neck. I've always loved them, even though they smelled like fish. But they made good money.

Lewis taught 'em how to work hard. They started their business in a tin shed, but now they have a nice buildin' to work in, with a big freezer.

I was standin' there lookin' at it when up walked 'is wife. She looked me in the eye and sed, "Lewis shore liked that house in Okahumpka, but he didn't wanna leave Tampa."

I knowed how he felt.

She went on to say, "He sold the house and built this buildin' to show to y'all, but then he got sick."

I sed, "It were 'is house to do with whatever he wanted to. I'm still glad I built it."

Sam's sister, Judy, come from Okahumpka with all them kids. They was a whole mess of 'em. The boys come by and sed, "That man that bought the house shore did like it. We built 'im a porch on the front and he lived in that house for 'bout a year afore he died. Then Jake Fussell from the lumber yard bought it. Jake knowed it were a good house 'cause he helped build it. Jake told me to thank y'all for the money y'all left at the lumber yard."

I told the family I were gonna rent me a room at the hotel, and asked Judy if'n I could rent a room for them.

But she sed, "No, this bunch'll sleep in their cars."

I told 'er, "I don't mind rentin' them a room."

But she jist sed, "See y'all tomorrow."

I slept hard and woke jist as the sun were comin' up. I like this time of day. I et in the restaurant. They didn't have no grits and eggs, but I made do.

I went back to the fish market. Judy done cooked for that whole bunch, and they was cleanin' up the place. They went to the bathroom to change clothes, and they looked like a different bunch of people.

I looked up and there stood Bill and 'is wife, Sarah. They had stopped to pick up John and Carla. I shore were proud of all of 'em. I went over to Bill and sed, "I shore am glad y'all made it. Lewis jist died in 'is sleep."

I cleaned up and changed clothes. The funeral were at 10. The preacher sed, "Lewis built the church that he were preachin' in." He told of all the good thangs that Lewis done. They sang a song and it were over.

I asked where they was gonna bury 'im. His wife sed, "Next to 'is mama. That's where he wanted to be."

I asked, "Want me to take' im back with me?" But they sed they would bring 'im, and sed he wouldn't smell for 'bout 5 days.

It were a fancy casket, not like Sam's. I started to leave, but John sed, "I'll drive y'all back, Dad. Come on, Carla. Y'all can drive Dad's truck."

Carla got in the truck and followed us to Homosassa. I shore am glad for both my boys.

When we got back to Homosassa it were 'bout dark. It'd been a long day. John and Carla slept at Clem and Sandy's. I went in and put my night clothes on and laid down. I slept all night and were up when the sun come up. That's the best time of day.

I stopped at Sally's to git me a cup of coffee. I looked out and all the boats was gone. I knowed they was goin', but didn't think that early.

I looked up and there stood Carla. I sed, "Carla, what time did they leave?"

She sed, "When we got home last night."

That sounded like somethin' I would do.

She told me she needed to go and fix her dad's lunch and sed, "I'll see y'all."

The Trip to John's

Chapter 37

It were Friday and I were settin' on the dock watchin' the boats go by. Some would blow their horn, and some jist waved.

I hadn't seen John in quite a while and thought I might jist go to Dade City for a little while. I stopped at Clem and Sandy's to see if'n she would like to go see 'er daughter, but she sed she couldn't go this time. Her 16-year-old daughter, Susan, heard me and sed, "I wanna go."

Sandy looked at me and sed, "You don't mind?"

I sed, "No, I'd love for 'er to go along."

The daughter sed, "I'll be ready in jist a little bit." And she ran in to pack a few thangs.

She were back in no time and had some stuff in a paper bag. We drove down Hwy 19, and I sed to her, "Wanna drive?"

She sed, "I don't know how; I never drove afore."

Sed, "I'll show y'all."

So I stopped the truck and we changed seats. She started the truck. I showed 'er where the gear were and how to let out the clutch. Well, it jumped and jumped, then it smoothed out. I told 'er to push on the clutch. I put it in 2nd gear and she done better.

We was doin' 'bout 25 miles an hour. Then she put it in high gear. It jumped quite a bit afore it smoothed out. She drove 'bout 35 miles an hour. She done a good job of drivin'.

James Carlton Fussell

When we got close to Dade City I told 'er, "I'll drive to John's."

We got to John's house and the ole brown dog were layin' on the porch. I knocked on the door, but nobody come to the door. Then Susan sed, "I hear somethin' runnin' over in them woods.

So I opened the gate and let 'er drive through it. It jumped real good through the gate, but everybody does that when they's learnin' to drive. I let 'er drive over to the woods. I seen the loader were clearin' land. So I told 'er to stop. We chugged to a stop and I laughed.

I looked at the loader and couldn't believe my eyes. They done built a box which that the little red-headed boy were ridin' in. It had a cage so the limbs wouldn't hit 'im.

Carla seen us and stopped the loader. She got off and hugged 'er sister. Then she climbed back on the loader to git 'er little red-headed boy. He looked like he'd been rootin' in the dirt.

I laughed and he jist smiled. Carla laughed and sed, "He'll ride all day in that box. If'n it has a motor in it, he likes it."

John seen 'er stop and come over to where we was at. He sed, "I shore am glad to see y'all."

Susan told Carla she drove to Dade City. John jist looked at me and smiled. Then John sed, "You shore do know how to make people happy."

I told 'em I couldn't stay long 'cause I wanted to git back home afore dark.

Susan looked at Carla and sed, "Can I stay here till Sunday?"

Carla sed, "I don't know why not."

So I sed, "Fine by me. I'll come git y'all on Sunday."

Then John sed, "No, we'll bring 'er back Sunday, 'bout 3 in the afternoon."

So I told Susan I'd tell 'er mama. I knowed Sandy wouldn't care.

Susan threw 'er arms 'round my neck and sed, "Thank you."

We all rode back to the house. That little red-headed boy rode in the back of the truck and Carla and Susan in the big ole truck. John rode with me. John sed, "I didn't understand what y'all was sayin' when y'all sed how much y'all love someone, till I married Carla. We work hard to clear all this land, but I wouldn't trade it for all the boats or anythin' else."

Sed, "I'm happy for y'all."

He sed, "We can't have no more kids. I'm sorry 'bout that, but I think that little red-headed boy will make up for it. Y'all know we named 'im after y'all, and call 'im 'Red,' like y'all."

That made me real happy.

John sed, "Bill and the local cattlemen are gonna give a big party for all the cattlemen in Florida at Bill's house. I told 'im I'd help 'im."

When we got to the house it were gittin' late, so I told them I'd see 'em on Sunday. Carla begged me to stay for supper, but I told 'er I needed to git on the road.

When I got back to Homosassa it were 'bout dark. I stopped at Sandy's to tell 'er Susan stayed at Carla's. She walked outside and jist laughed. She sed, "I knowed that was what y'all was gonna do. I think they both need to git together sometimes."

I told 'er they was workin' real hard, but they was gonna bring Susan back 'bout 3 on Sunday. I sed, "Carla's little red-headed boy looked like he'd been rootin' in the dirt, and he rides in that front end loader with Carla all the time."

Clem come outside. He wanted to know how Carla were doin'. I told 'im, "She's doin' jist fine. They's gonna have a big ranch some day."

Then I told 'em, "Think I'll go to the restaurant and get me a bite to eat."

I walked inside and told Sally I'd like a glass of milk and some cracklin' cornbread. She shore do make good cornbread. I et it all and that filled me up. I had a glass of tea, too. Guess that'll keep me up all night, but that's alright.

Well, the weekend went by fast and here it were, Sunday afternoon already. I looked up from the dock and here come Bill. Guess John called 'im. Sed, "I sure am glad to see y'all, Bill. Where's the boys?"

He sed, "Workin' on the fence over on Long Ranch. They work all the time, but they still throw cow poop at each other."

Then here come John and Carla bringin' Susan back. Carla done bought Susan new boots, new shirt, hat and ridin' pants. She shore looked nice in 'em.

They all walked down to the dock where Bill and I was settin'. That little red-headed boy walked up to Bill and sed, "I'm Red Fussell." Bill jist laughed.

Bill sed, "He looks like 'im, too." And we all laughed.

Bill told me he were gonna have a big party, and I could invite all the Fussell bunch and Sandy and Clem's bunch. Nobody needs to bring nothin'.

I told 'im, "Well, they can bring what they wanna bring."

Then I asked Bill if'n I could bring Earl, the tax collector.

He sed, "Shore. He ain't a bad feller."

Bill told us that 'bout a week ago he drove to Tampa and stopped at the fish market. He sed, "It covers 'bout a whole block, with the biggest ice plant I ever seen. They give me a lot of fish. Them girls was still cleanin' fish, but they smell like money. Lewis woulda been proud of 'em. All them kids was cleanin' fish. Guess it's the biggest fish market in Florida. He told me, "They really got goin' when they sold the house y'all give to Lewis. That's when they bought all that land for the fish market."

I sed, "I shore am glad they's doin' good. They work real hard."

Then Bill told me he had a crew comin' to help John clear off 'is ranch. I'm not shore I'da did that, but if'n he wants to help out, I'm shore John will like that.

Then John come up and sed, "Carla shore were glad to see 'er sister. They laughed and then they cried. They laughed 'bout their mama puttin' a switch on them. When one did somethin' wrong, she switched 'em all."

We all jist laughed.

I shore were proud of my boys. I told John and Bill, "I'm gonna give Sandy's girls 10 gold coins and my grandkids 30 gold coins. You 2 can split the rest. You both know where they's at. And I want one in my hand when y'all bury me."

John sed they needed to git on the road. So he went to Carla's mother and give 'er a hug and then 'er dad, 'er sister and then me. And they headed back to Dade City.

The Boat Trip

Chapter 38

I got up early and went to Sally's for breakfast. When I finished, one of them boat captains come over to me as asked if'n I'd like to go shrimpin' today. Sed they would be back tonight.

I sed, "Shore would."

He told me not to bring food; they'd have plenty to eat. I could jist come as I were.

We walked down to the dock. It were jist like old times. I started to walk out front, but he sed to come inside. He handed me the key to the boat. Then he sed, "Y'all take 'er to the Gulf."

I took 'er through Hell's Gate, left, 2 rights, 2 lefts, right. We left marker #2 indicatin' the last marker afore shore, and the compass were right at 280, headin' to some good rocks.

Then he sed, "When y'all think we's in the right place, drop the nets."

I looked at the water. When it looked right, I lowered the nets. We run for 'bout an hour and then raised 'em. We made a good run and got quite a bunch of shrimp. The crew boys cleaned the deck. I looked at the captain and sed, "This here's y'all's boat. I'll let y'all make the next run."

So he sed, "Well, y'all run the boat. I'll lower the net."

I felt 20 years younger. It felt real good. It's hard work, and if'n y'all make a mistake it could ruin y'all's whole day.

We run 'bout 2 hours and then raised the net. He were a good boat captain. All 'is crew worked hard. We stopped the boat and et lunch. This shore made me 'member what real hard work were.

Then the captain sed, "Take 'er to the dock."

When I went by marker # 2, I thought Sam would be lookin' for me. I shore miss 'er.

I pulled the boat up to the dock. I felt good all over and thanked the captain. I told 'im I shore had a good day.

He sed, "Y'all git y'all's pay on Friday."

I laughed and sed, "Y'all mean I have to pay y'all."

We both laughed. He give me a big ole bag of shrimp, but I sed, "Give 'em to the crew."

He sed, "No. Y'all earned 'em."

I thanked 'im again for a good day and left the boat.

I seen Susan outside. She washed dishes at Sally's restaurant sometimes. I hollered at 'er and she stopped. I give 'er the shrimp. She hugged me. That made me feel good.

Then she sed, "If'n y'all go to Dade City, I wanna go."

Bad Trip to Inverness

Chapter 39

The sun were almost up, so I stopped to git me a cup of coffee, and then I watched the sun on the water. I watched the boats leave sometimes and wished I were goin' to the Gulf, but I knowed I were jist too old.

I seen Sandy comin' and knowed somethin' were wrong. She were cryin'. I asked 'er what were wrong and she sed, "I got trouble and don't know what to do 'bout it."

I sed, "Is it Clem?"

But she sed, "No. He's a good man and he works real hard. It's my 20-year-old daughter, Barbara, in Inverness. Her husband give 'er a black eye. She has one child and is gonna have another one. I jist don't know what to do 'bout it."

Sed, "Go git y'all's pocketbook. We're goin' to Inverness."

I didn't drive real fast, but this time it were faster than I do most of the time. We got to Inverness, and I asked Sandy if'n she knowed where they lived. She warn't shore, but had the address.

We drove up to the house. I wouldn't even let my chickens live in that there house!

Sandy walked inside and 'er daughter cried. I told Sandy to tell Barbara to go git what she needed and come with us. Barbara sed, "He'll beat me if'n I leave."

But I told 'er to not worry 'bout that.

We loaded up what she wanted. Then I asked 'er where she'd like to go. She sed, "If'n Carla will have me, I'd like to go there."

I looked at Sandy and then back to Barbara and sed, "I know she'd take y'all with open arms."

She sed, "Carla sends me money all the time. A lot of times we wouldn't have nothin' to eat if'n it warn't for 'er." Then she cried again.

We had a truckload up in the front seat, but it didn't take long afore we was in Dade City. We drove right to John's ranch. I walked up to the house and knocked on the door. Carla opened the door to see 'er mother and 'er sister with me. She grabbed 'er sister and hugged 'er, then Sandy sed, "Carla, Barbara has no place to go. She needs a place to live."

Carla looked Barbara and sed, "As long as I have a place to live, y'all have a place to live."

Barbara sed, "What will John say?"

Carla sed, "Well, he would be mad at me if'n I didn't take y'all in!"

John seen my truck. He hurried to the house and sed, "Anythin' wrong?"

He looked at Barbara and sed, "Who done this?"

I spoke up and sed, "He beat 'er for the last time. She has no place to go."

John sed, "She can stay here as long as she wants to."

"I've gotta go make a phone call."

He called the police in Inverness and told them what happened, and he wanted it fixed so 'er husband couldn't come to 'is house. Then he called the Dade City police and told them the same thang. He didn't want that man hangin' 'round.

They sed they'd take care of it and wanted a picture of what he done to 'er. So they sent a man out to take 'er picture.

After they left I asked John how he got the police to act so quick, and he sed, "I give them a cow to cook to help 'em buy a new car for the department."

Carla's red-headed boy, little Red, and Barbara's little girl, Patty, was 'bout the same age. So they was gonna move little Red's stuff to a small room in the back.

Barbara sed, "I don't wanna jist take 'is room." She looked at little

Red and sed, "Can I have y'all's room?"

He jist looked at 'er and smiled. He sed, "I love y'all," and he started movin' 'is stuff out to the small room.

Sandy started to move little Red's bed, but Carla sed, "No, leave it here. Red likes to sleep in the dresser drawer."

Sandy laughed and sed, "I bet y'all wouldn't let 'im."

Carla sed, "Y'all're right, but now he can do it."

I took Sandy back to Homosassa after Barbara were settled.

The next day Carla took Barbara to the store and bought Patty, the unborn baby, and 'er some new clothes. Barbara sed, "Don't do this. I don't wanna make John mad at me."

But Carla sed, "He's the one that told me to do it."

Then it happened! Barbara's husband walked up to them in the store. He told 'er if'n she didn't go back with 'im, he'd beat 'er till she lost the new baby." But 'bout that time, up walked the police chief.

Carla sed, "That's the one that beat 'er, and he told 'er it'd be worse the next time."

The police sed to the man, "Walk outside." The police chief told 'im somethin' he didn't wanna hear.

Barbara's husband sed, "Yes, Sir. No, I won't do nothin'. I'm leavin' and I won't be back."

He got in 'is old junk car and drove off. Carla asked the police what he told 'im. The police sed, "I told 'im, if'n he ever touched 'er again, I would give 'im to the KKK and that would be the last of 'im."

Carla sed, "Let's go get us an ice cream."

Her sister sed, "Why are y'all doin' all this for me?"

Carla sed, "A long time ago, when the Fussells come to Homosassa, they was a man named Ray, and he told Red Fussell, 'Never be greedy. If'n y'all can help somebody, do it.' So we all try to do somethin' to help if'n we can."

They stopped to git ice cream. Barbara sed, "My! It shore is good."

When they went to pay, the woman at the register sed, "It's on the house."

Carla thanked 'er.

Then Barbara sed, "Why didn't she charge y'all?"

Carla sed, "At one time the lady that runs the ice cream store had no job and no money. We loaned 'er the money to start the store. She worked hard and paid us back. Now she makes a good livin' sellin' ice cream. In the winter she makes donuts and sells coffee and hot chocolate."

One day Barbara asked Carla, "Do y'all have a sewin' machine?" She sed she did.

So Barbara asked 'er if'n she would buy 'er some cloth to make some clothes. So Carla took 'er to the cloth store in Dade City and told the lady what she needed. She got quite a bit of cloth. Then the store keeper told Carla she had a bolt of cloth she couldn't sell. It were tan cotton, but were real heavy.

They put the cloth in the car. They looked up. There stood 'er husband and 2 of 'is friends. They was all drunk.

He sed, "I'll jist take y'all back to Inverness now. Then if'n them Fussells come there, I'll beat the tar out of 'em."

Carla didn't know it, but the police seen 'em come back in town. One of 'em bad guys sed, "I'm leavin' here. Them Fussells, no tellin' what they'd do to me." And he left.

The police grabbed the other 2. Well, I don't know what he done to 'em, but I hear tell they won't be back.

Carla and 'er sister drove back home. Her sister sed, 'I hate that I got y'all in trouble, but I jist had no place to go."

Carla sed, "They will always be trouble, but y'all have to know that the Fussells will always do what is right, and everybody knows it."

They unloaded the cloth. John come in and Carla told 'im they'd have supper fixed soon. They set down to eat, and John sed the blessin' and prayed. "Thank y'all, God, for sendin' Carla's sister to stay with us."

Little Red were actin' up so Carla tapped 'im on the head with a spoon and he shut up.

The next mornin' Barbara had breakfast fixed. She's a good cook. Her mama taught 'er real good. John started to leave the house after he were done eatin', and seen Bill and a crew of men comin' through the gate with all kinds of equipment to clear land. Bill's 2 boys, Kyle and Nick, was with 'em.

Kyle come runnin' to the house to tell 'is Aunt Carla they would be 10 hungry men at noon time. Them boys shore has growed up. John told Carla to go to Homosassa and git plenty of fish.

They left for Homosassa and got there in no time. I were sittin' on the dock and they sed they needed lots of fish to feed that bunch that were clearin' land. Carla stopped at 'er mama's house, too, to say, "Hi," afore they left. They took shrimp and fish and ice with 'em back to Dade City.

They took the wash pot and filled it with lard. Then they built a good fire and got it hot, but not too hot. They cooked a big pot of grits and made plenty of cracklin' cornbread. They got the ice out of the ice box. John done made it so ice wouldn't melt too fast.

They cooked the fish and some shrimp. When it were all cooked, they took a cloth and strained the lard back into the lard can to be used again.

When it were time for lunch, Carla went to the horn and pulled the string. She blowed 2 shorts and 1 long. She could hear them shut off all the machines.

Here they come to lunch. They set lunch out on the porch. They had sweet tea. Carla done made strong tea; that's how John likes it. They looked up and here I come with Clem and Sandy. We wasn't gonna miss out on a good meal.

That shore made Carla happy. She hugged 'er dad and mom and then me. Them cowboys washed in the cow trough afore comin' to eat. Carla put some soap and a rag to dry their faces and hands out there, too.

John sed the blessin'. I watched to see if'n little Red needed to git tapped on the head with a spoon again, but he didn't need it today.

They all got 'em a plate and filled it full. Carla saved some of the lard to put on the grits, and they had a big glass of sweet tea. If'n I drank a glass of that tea, I wouldn't sleep for a week.

When they was all full, some of 'em laid on the porch, and some of 'em set under the tree. And that ole brown dog, he were full, too.

Afore long it were time for them to go back to work. They all thanked Carla and Barbara for the good meal. Sandy sed she would do the clean up, but the girls jist laughed and sed, "Sounds jist like 'er, don't it?"

When the kitchen were all cleaned, Sandy thanked Carla for takin' 'er sister in. Carla looked at 'er mama and sed, "I'd take y'all in, too, if'n y'all needed me."

Sandy told Clem they needed to git back home, so the 3 of us climbed back in the car and went back to Homosassa. It were 'bout dark.

Carla went down where they was workin' to tell Bill, "I still got a lot of fish left, if'n they'd eat 'em."

Bill sed, "I'll ask them."

As the workers started to leave everybody got somethin' to eat and drink, even the ole brown dog.

They put the kids to bed, and then set out on the screened-in-porch. That screen shore did keep them skeeters off.

Barbara sed, "I never knowed people lived like this. This were fun, but it were hard work."

They set for a while and then she sed, "I were shore glad to see Mama and Daddy. They mean a lot to me."

John were tired and sed, "I'm gonna go to bed. We cleared 'bout 40 acres today. Shore glad I have a good brother."

The next mornin' they et breakfast 'bout 6. This would be another day of hard work. Barbara asked if'n she could have an old pair of John's pants. Carla got a pair that had a hole in 'em."

Carla asked 'er if'n she would look after little Red while she worked outside, and Barbara sed, "Shore."

Carla told 'er, "If'n he needs 'is behind warmed up, jist do it."

But little Red had someone to play with. He and Patty fussed at each other some, but if'n she got tired of 'im, she'd jist bite 'im. She'd bite hard enough for 'im to really know it.

Carla went to Dade City to take care of some ranch business. While she were there she talked to a builder to see if'n they would build a house real close to them. Then she bought a new sewin' machine that would sew on heavy cloth. On the way back, she stopped to get an ice cream, but the ice cream shop were closed. She seen a note on the door and went up to read it. The ice cream lady died the day afore. That made 'er sad.

She come on home and told her sister that the ice cream woman died, and showed her the new sewin' machine and heavy thread. Barbara's eyes got big as saucers.

The next 2 days Barbara closed the door, and she sewed all day long while she took care of the kids. On Friday, she told John and Carla to close their eyes. She had somethin' for them.

Then she told 'em to open their eyes. There stood little Red dressed in a ranch hand's suit, with a dark green shirt and ridin' britches, with the flair on the sides so the thorns and bushes wouldn't hurt 'im. And he had on 'is boots. He looked real good, like he were ready to punch cows.

Then she give John 'is pants and shirt to try on. And she give Carla an apron that she done put lace around.

John come out. He looked good. She done put a watch pocket in 'is pants so he wouldn't lose 'is watch. John's pants had that flair on the sides, too, and the bottoms laced up to keep the dirt out.

He done wore 'is new pants and shirt to the cow meetin' in Inverness. At the meetin' the cowboys shore did like 'em pants and wanted to know where he got 'em. He told 'em Carla's sister made 'em. They wanted to know what she'd charge to make some for them.

John really didn't know, but thought 'bout 18 dollars. "She'll need a pair of y'all's old pants for size. Jist bring them to my house in Dade City." They really like the flair on the sides to keep them thorn bushes off 'em.

Barbara made Carla a jacket, too. It looked real nice.

Then Barbara told Carla that the baby were comin' out. So Carla rushed 'er to the doctor's office. That baby were really here! It were a girl.

Little Red wanted a baby boy to play with 'im and Patty. But Carla picked 'er up and sed, "Ain't she cute!"

Then Barbara told Carla, "I named 'er after y'all, Carla Annette Fussell." She told Carla she wanted to change from 'er married name to Fussell, if'n it were okay with 'er.

Carla sed, "Y'all shore can."

And she did. She got John to help 'er with the paperwork and become a Fussell a month later.

New Shop in Dade City

Chapter 40

John told Carla he had to go to Dade City for a while. He stayed nearly all day, but when he come home he sed he done bought the ice cream shop, the whole block and the buildin'. He were gonna have it all redone.

He sed, "That way Barbara will have a place close by, and she can make them ridin' britches and sell 'em, and sell hats and boots, too. Them's all thangs cattlemen need. We might even sell cars."

Carla jist looked at 'im and sed, "And who's gonna do all that work?"

He sed, "Y'all."

Carla sed, "Well, who's gonna wash y'all's clothes and cook y'all's meals?"

He jist laughed and sed, "Did y'all jist turn y'all's nose up?" But Carla didn't think it were funny.

Carla helped Barbara with the new baby, and Barbara were makin' pants for 2 cowboys. It were a big order.

The builder started on Barbara's house. It were gonna be a real nice house, but Barbara didn't know it were 'ers. Then when John told 'er he bought the place in Dade City to open a shop for 'er she cried.

He sed, "Y'all're gonna need some help. They's a real big order for some of 'em pants. Them cowboys like 'em."

The Mullet Boys

The more she made, the better she got at it.

Carla done told John she warn't gonna go run no shop, nose turned up or not. But he really didn't want 'er to; he were jist rufflin' 'er feathers, and doin' a good job of it.

John asked Barbara if'n she could run the ice cream place along with the clothin' store. She didn't know, but sed she'd be willin' to try.

Carla knowed what John were doin'. He thought she'd go down and help 'er, but that warn't gonna happen!

They bought 5 more sewin' machines from a place in New York. They had all kinds of cloth. John told Barbara when they bought the sewin' machines, she'd need to teach the workers how to use 'em when they got to Dade City.

John done got in touch with a hat company, and they sent 'im a book full of hats with their prices and all kinds of cloth and boots.

He had a table made to put stuff on, and he made a sign that sed they needed help from anyone who knowed how to sew and sell ice cream.

Again Carla sed, "I don't want nothin' to do with this."

Barbara didn't know what were goin' on, but she were makin' 'em pants and gittin' more orders than she could fill. Seemed everyone wanted a pair of them pants. They should last forever, and when they rode horses, it would keep them thorns off 'em. They looked real good.

Her baby girl were growin' fast. Everyone loved 'er, even little Red. He sed he liked 'er 'cause she didn't bite.

John bought hats, shoes, boots and cloth. He had a store full and hired a bunch of people. Barbara were teachin' them how to sew on 'em new sewin' machines. They shore run smooth and Barbara shore could sew good. They had lots of cloth, 'bout anythin' anyone would want.

He hired a lady to run the cloth shop and order all the cloth. They was gonna open on Friday, so they needed to price the cloth and shoes.

Them women was makin' them rider pants and sold a bunch of patterns for all kinds of clothes.

When they opened the door on Friday, they was lots of people. So they jist gave ice cream away, even to the kids in the neighborhood, and they et a bunch of it. Barbara collected money all day long. Them Stetson hats warn't cheap, but they's a good hat.

John thought maybe Carla would come by, but she were takin' care of the kids at home. She wanted nothin' to do with no store!

John spend 'bout 2,000 dollars to put all this stuff in the store, and the first day they sold 1,985 dollars worth, and still had a bunch of stuff left. They had to order more hats and boots. Them ranch hands ordered pants, and farmers wanted 'em with no flair on the side. The sewin' machines never stopped all day long.

Bill come by and sed, "What in the world have y'all started now?"

Barbara sed, "Bill, I made y'all somethin' special." And she handed 'im a shirt.

He looked at the shirt. It had a pocket on each side and it were heavy cloth with long sleeves and brass buttons. It had a big collar so he could turn it up to keep the sun off 'is neck. He put it on and sed, "I'll have to wear it in the winter, when it's cooler."

The next day were jist as busy. John placed a new order and jist hoped the new stuff got there real quick. It made it in 2 days and they made 3,000 dollars, and cleared 1,000 dollars.

Then a man from Tampa stopped by. When he seen how busy they was, he asked if'n they'd sell the business.

John looked at Barbara and they went into the office to talk 'bout it. John sed they had 'bout 2,000 dollars in everythin' and suggested they ask for 5,000 dollars. He told 'er that if'n the man give them 5,000 dollars, she would have 3,000, and she could still make them pants at home.

The store were full of people, and the prices was good for them to buy. It were good stuff.

John told the Tampa man they would sell it for 5,000 dollars, minus the sewin' machines. And he showed 'im how much they made in 2 days.

But the man sed that price were too high, so John jist sed, "Then don't buy it." And John started to walk out the door.

The man sed, "I'll give that for it."

The next day he come back with the money. John told 'im the buildin' didn't go with it, and the rent would be 100 dollars a month. The man agreed that would be fine.

John told Barbara 'er husband would want part of it if'n he learned she had the shop. They checked, and shore 'nuff, they found 'im in Tampa again.

John took a lawyer to Tampa and found Barbara's husband. They asked 'im when he were gonna pay Barbara for support for the baby. He sed, "Never."

So they give 'im papers to sign that sed he wanted nothin' she had, or would ever have. If'n he didn't sign it, John were gonna have 'im put in jail. He finally signed it, without even readin' it. The lawyer had it all down in print where he could never touch nothin'.

John and the lawyer went back to Dade City. When they was through with the new store owner, John had a check for Barbara for 3,000 dollars.

When John got home Barbara were settin' up the new sewin' machines in the spare room. John sed, "Y'all're puttin' 'em in the wrong house."

She looked at 'im and sed, "What do y'all mean?"

John jist told 'er, "Go ask Carla."

Carla laughed. She sed, "I'll tell y'all tomorrow."

John give 'er the check for 3,000 dollars. She looked back and forth between John and Carla, and then she cried. John told 'er it were 'ers to use however she wanted to. She sed, "But this is y'all's money, not mine."

Carla sed, "It's y'all's now, to do whatever y'all please."

John told 'er 'bout 'is trip to Tampa and the paper 'er husband signed.

The next day Carla took 'er down to 'er new house. They took little Red and Patty with 'em. Little Red didn't mess with Patty much no more. She'd bite 'im if'n he started gittin' the best of 'er. The house shore were nice. Patty run from room to room and seen one room that were pink. She sed, "This here's my room!"

Barbara asked Carla, "How much is this house?"

Carla sed, "I don't know. Y'all will have to ask John."

John jist sed, "It's free. We's jist glad we can do it."

John stopped by the store one day. All the help he hired were gone. They was 2 women sewin', but they wasn't doin' a good job. The place warn't clean, and the new owner had cheap stuff with a high price. He done shut down the ice cream. They were no customers in the shop. One of the help told 'im she hadn't been paid in 2 weeks, and today were 'er last day.

James Carlton Fussell

John left. He hadn't gotten 'is rent money for 2 months neither, and he were thinkin' the man were gonna close the doors. He stopped by 2 weeks later and everythin' were gone, 'cept the ice cream machine and a table. The place shore were a mess. He hired 2 ladies to clean it up, but he didn't really want Barbara to open it back up.

He told Barbara what happened to the shop and that he didn't really want 'er to open it back up. He told 'er she could make a good livin' right there makin' them pants that 'em cowboys was wearin'. She agreed.

Her baby were growin' fast and little Red shore did like 'er. He showed John where Patty bit 'im.

John jist laughed.

My Move to Inverness

Chapter 41

The girls at the restaurant called Bill and told 'im he needed to come and git me. All I done was cry all day. I jist miss Sam so much.

Bill called John to meet 'im in Homosassa and told 'im they needed to move me. Bill sed, "We can move 'im to my house in Inverness."

They both got here 'bout the same time and told me I had to go live with Bill. I jist looked at the boys and sed, "Ok, if'n I can come back sometimes."

They asked what I wanted to do with my house. I jist told 'em, "I'll let y'all know."

They loaded up most of my stuff. I went to tell the girls at the restaurant, "I'm leavin'."

When I come back, I told the boys that I done give my house to 'em at the restarant. They's always good to me.

I told John to git the box out from under the house. Then I told 'em it were full of the gold Sam and I found. I told 'em the story again 'bout the shoe with the map in it and reminded 'em that's why they was rich. And I 'minded 'em of what Ray always sed, "Never be greedy". I told 'em I always tried to do the right thang.

I looked at John and asked how 'is little red-headed boy were doin'. Bill sed, "He's jist like y'all." We all laughed.

James Carlton Fussell

John drove 'is truck over and filled it with what he wanted. Bill told John he were gonna build a room at the back of 'is house and sed, "When my boy, Steve, gets outa school, he can look after 'im."

John sed, "I'll pay for it."

But Bill sed, "No. Someday I might need another room."

We all got in Bill's truck and went to Inverness. Steve shore were glad to see me.

I done give all my grandsons pearl-handled .38 pistols and a right and left holster.

They put all my stuff in the back bedroom. I called Bill and John in and told 'em I wanted to be buried on Shell Island with Sam. John looked at Bill and sed, "Did y'all know that?"

Bill sed, "Yes, I did."

Bill took John back to 'is truck in Homosassa, and John sed, "I'll come to see 'im every chance I get." And he left for Dade City.

The Train Wreck

Chapter 42

John had jist shut down the front end loader when he heard 2 shorts and 1 long blast. Then it sounded again. He rushed home to find Carla cryin'. She sed, "John, my dad got kilt on the railroad in Green Swamp."

John sed, "Get little Red ready. I'll go git your sister and 'er family. It may take a little time to git the girls ready."

He knocked on Barbara's door and told 'er, 'er dad had been kilt on the railroad.

She burst into tears.

John sed, "We need to git thangs together. We's goin' to Homosassa as soon as we can git ready."

John went back to the house to pick up Carla and little Red, then went back to pick up Barbara and the kids. They had a car full. The kids was real good. They knowed somethin' were wrong.

They got to Homosassa in 'bout 45 minutes. Sandy were so upset. They sed a rail fell on 3 men when they went to unload the rails.

I went to Green Swamp jist as soon as I heard. When I got there one of the men that worked for Clem sed, "The brakeman and the engineer had been fussin' all day. The engine shook and the rail fell on all 3 of 'em."

Well, there weren't nothin' I could do to help, so I come back. They had the funeral on Friday at the church. They buried Clem next to the railroad track. He always loved trains.

The girls told Sandy she needed to move to Dade City, where they lived. Clem and Sandy was jist rentin' the house in Homosassa anyhow. She could jist pull up and move.

So, 2 weeks later, Sandy moved to Dade City. We all helped move 'er stuff in 'bout 3 loads. She moved in with Barbara. They put the little girls in one room and Sandy moved into the larger room, but she sed she wouldn't be there long. Carla told 'er they was gonna build 'er a house down the road.

Little Red called 'er, "Grandma Red."

She sed, "Red, my name's Grandma Sandy."

He jist smiled. As they went down the road he sed, "Bye, Grandma Red." And he sed it over and over again.

Sandy sed, "I'd better git me a good switch. I know I'm gonna need one." Them girls jist laughed.

Monday mornin' John left for Tampa to see a lawyer. He weren't gonna let the railroad not pay Sandy somethin'. When he got back in Dade City he told Sandy she would get 5,000 dollars from the railroad.

Sandy told Carla that she now had enough of her own money to build 'er house, but Carla jist laughed. They started to build the house the next week.

Carla told 'er Barbara weren't gonna let er sew 'em pants and shirts, but Sandy sed she'd like to, 'cause when she were sewin' little Red set on 'er lap jist to watch 'er sew. She let 'im cut the thread and try to thread the needle. But every time he left 'er at the sewin' machine he'd say, "Bye, Grandma Red." Sandy would shake 'er fist at 'im and when he were gone she laughed.

The little girls was learnin' how to sew, too. Time were passin' real fast. The shirt and pants business was growin' big. They done built a big buildin' out back. Sandy's house were finished and she were now moved in.

Trip to Bill's

Chapter 43

Sometime later on a Saturday, John told young Red they was gonna go see Red Fussell. Red wanted to know if'n 'is sisters could go, too.

John sed, "Shore. But go ask their mama."

They was in the truck ready to go. It were a bit crowded, but they didn't care.

When they got to Bill's, and afore they even got out of the truck, young Red asked 'is dad, "Is that my sister's grandpa, too?"

John sed, "Shore it is."

When they got to Bill's they got out of the truck. The girls went right to me and hugged my neck. I shore did like it.

Young Red sed, "Hi, Grandpa. I ain't a gonna hug y'all like 'em girls done. I'm way too big now." But I grabbed 'im and rubbed my whiskers across 'is face.

Bill laughed and sed, "Them red heads done meet their match!"

The girls went inside where Sarah were cookin'. They wanted to help, so Sarah had them set the table. No one were lazy. Everyone worked. That way thangs git done.

I told Bill to go git the box under 'is bed. They was 2 pearl-handled pistols with holsters. Young Red's eyes got big as they could get. I told 'im, "Never point the gun at anythin' y'all don't wanna kill. And don't never point it at anyone when y'all're mad."

I showed 'im how to shoot. Then I told Steve to go git some shells. I loaded the gun and showed young Red how to look through the sight and then how to squeeze the trigger. I asked 'im, "Do you want to shoot it?"

He did, of course. He didn't tell me he already knowed all this, and I didn't know John had been teachin' 'im for a long time. They had a pipe they shot at all the time, and it would ring when they hit it. This here pistol were a 8-shot pistol.

Young Red were ready to shoot. He loaded both guns like a pro. That pipe were in trouble. Young Red hit the pipe on all 8 shots, ping, ping, ping, ping, ping, ping, ping, ping. He looked to make shore the gun were unloaded and handed it back to me, but I sed, "They's y'all's."

His eyes got big as saucers. I sed, "Can y'all shoot a rifle?"

Young Red sed, "Shore can."

So I had Steve go git my rifle. It were an old gun and I handed it to 'im. That young red-headed boy loaded that rifle. It were a lever-action rifle. The wind were a blowin', but he shot all 8 bullets and hit the pipe every time.

I looked at 'im and sed, "Well, y'all can have the rifle, too."

Young Red looked at Steve and could tell, even at 'is age, that Steve really wanted it. So he thought a minute, and then he sed, "Grandpa, y'all give me this rifle. Can I give it to somebody?"

Well, I looked at 'im and sed, "I guess so." But I were hurt that he didn't want to keep it.

But young Red made shore it didn't have no more shells in it and walked over to Steve and handed it to 'im. He sed, "Steve, y'all can have it."

I had tears in my eyes, and I sed, "Steve, I didn't know y'all wanted it."

Steve tried to give it back, but it were where it belonged. Bill were watchin' what were goin' on and sed, "Steve, Ray told Grandpa, 'Don't be greedy.'" I guess it's in the Fussell family.

It were time for lunch. Sarah done fixed a good lunch. The girls helped 'er and we all set down and et. Bill's 2 older boys showed up. They et everythin' 'cept the table cloth, and drank up some kind of tea. They'd been wormin' the cows and cuttin' the horns. It were hard work but they knowed how. Bill looked at John and sed, "It's all been hard work, but we done it."

John told the girls it were time to go, but they sed they had to clean the kitchen. He sed, "Ok."

John walked out with Bill and went to look at 'is new bull. He looked like a nice one. He told me he paid 500 dollars for 'im, which were a good price. John told Bill, "If'n y'all need any help with our dad, jist call me."

The girls come outside. They was ready to go home. I called the girls over and give 'em somethin', and they started back to Dade City.

One of the girls showed John a 50-dollar gold piece. John thought, *Dad's at it again. Them girls love 'im and it shows he loves them.*

Young Red's at It Again

Chapter 44

John got a call from the school. They'd been some trouble there. Young Red whipped up on a boy that made fun of one of 'em girls that didn't have much. He'd done made 'er some clothes.

The other boy sed somethin' young Red didn't like, so he give 'im a black eye. The teacher told John the boy were makin' fun of 'er, and Red took care of it. But she went on to say, "We can't have that behavior here."

The principal got in the middle of it and called Red to 'is office, with John and the teacher. The principal sed, "Red, I'm gonna beat on the desk, and when I do, you holler real loud. And everytime I hit it, you holler again. Can y'all make a tear?" Young Red left the office lookin' like he'd had a whippin' put on 'im. Inside he were laughin', but cryin' on the outside.

The principal told John, "He's jist like 'is granddad. They's two peas in a pod."

John took young Red back to the ranch. They laughed all the way back.

Sandy come out to see what were goin' on, and sed, "If'n he needs another whippin', I'll give it to 'im!" Then she laughed. Red told 'is grandma what went on at school that day and they all laughed again.

A Good Lesson

Chapter 45

Time were a-passin' fast. Young Red were now 12 years old, and he still tried to set on Grandma's lap, but now he were doin' the sewin' and Grandma Red were cuttin' the thread.

Grandma Red had 'bout wore out 10 of 'em switches on 'is behind, but he loved 'er. The girls was sewin' too. They was turnin' out lots of clothes.

When young Red would leave the sewin' room, Grandma would point her finger at 'im and then he'd say, "Bye, Grandma Red." And he laughed. She did too.

When anyone would ask 'bout the girls, young Red would say, "Them's my sisters."

They all rode horses. None of 'em smoked or chewed tobacco. Good thang, Grandma Red would skin their behinds. They all worked real hard and they made their own clothes now.

The kids at school liked the clothes they made. The Fussels seemed to dress better than most of the kids. They was a poor family that lived 'bout a mile down the road. They's clothes didn't look so good and the kids at school made fun of 'em.

One day young Red got by himself. He were sewin' somethin', but Sandy told the family to jist let 'im be. Every afternoon when he were

James Carlton Fussell

out of school, he were sewin'. Then one day, he asked Grandma Sandy if'n she would make the button holes.

She sed, "Shore." She looked at what he done, and it were good. So she sed, "Who are y'all makin' this for?"

He sed, "They's a family at school that don't have much and the other kids make fun of their ragged clothes. I jist don't like it, so I made some clothes for 'em.

A tear come to Sandy's eyes and she sed, "Do they have shoes?"

He sed, "No."

Somehow, Sandy found out what size shoes they wore and got 'em all new shoes. Then Sandy had them come to 'er house and had the girls fix their hair. They never had their hair fixed afore.

They went to school the next day and everybody turned and looked at 'em. They was real good-lookin' girls.

They was 'bout 12 girls. One of the girls walked up to young Red and kissed 'im on the cheek. His heart jist fluttered.

He told Grandma Red all 'bout it, and she jist smiled and thought, *He's jist like 'is grandpa.*

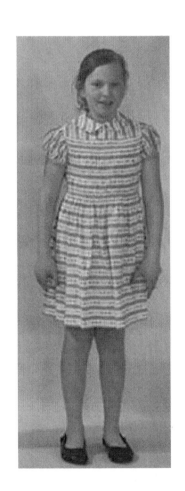

Graduation

Chapter 46

Time were goin' fast. Young Red were now in 'is last year of school. He and 'is sister, Patty, was graduatin'. Grandma asked 'im what he were gonna do when he graduated, and he sed, "I'm gonna go to Texas to be a Texas Ranger."

She sed, "No, I don't want y'all to go."

He sed, "But, Grandma, that's what I always wanted to do."

She sed, "Have y'all told y'all's mama?"

He sed, "No, but I'll tell 'er today."

Grandma sed, "I'm still not gonna like it. What'd y'all's dad say?"

Sed, "He told me if'n that were what I wanted to do, to jist do it."

The day school were out, Red loaded up 'is truck, took 'is guns and all the clothes 'is grandma done made 'im. He were gonna go to Houston to apply for ranger school. He thought he'd have a good chance of gittin' in cause 'is grades was good.

He sed, "Goodbye" to 'is mama and dad. His sisters give 'im a kiss. He shore loved 'em girls. Then there stood Grandma Red. She grabbed 'im and cried all over 'im. Then she told 'im to be careful and not take no chances. Red told 'er he loved 'er.

Grandma sed, "I got a good mind to go with y'all!" They all laughed. Carla sed, "The front seat is full. You'll have to ride in the back."

Grandma shooked 'er fist at Carla and laughed.

When Red were drivin' down the road, Grandma Red were jist a cryin'. Carla put 'er arm around 'er and Grandma sed, "Y'all shouldna let 'im go."

Texas Ranger School

Chapter 47

Young Red got to Texas in jist 2 days. He slept in 'is tent to save 'is money. He didn't know what would happen if'n he called home. He shore didn't wanna to talk to 'is grandma yet; he were shore she'd tell 'im to come back home.

He went to the main office to apply to be a ranger. When they asked 'is name he sed, "Red Fussell."

One of the men looked at 'im and sed, "Are y'all from Homosassa, Florida?"

He sed, "No, but my grandpa were."

The man sed, "We knowed your grandpa years ago." He went on to tell 'im that he would have 8 weeks of school and it warn't gonna be easy.

Red sed, "Jist when do I start?"

They sed, "The state will pay for y'all's school. If'n y'all don't pass, y'all will be gone. We'll give y'all a place to stay. They's 20 in the class, and half will flunk out for all kinds of reasons."

Red asked, "Can I use my own guns?"

He sed, "Let me see 'em."

Red showed 'im both guns and the man asked, "Can y'all hit the target with 'em?"

Sed, "Shore."

He sed, "They's a range out there. Let's go see what y'all can do."
They was havin' class but he walked in the class. He told the teacher,
"See what this boy can do." He told Red to load 'is gun.

Red sed, "Both of 'em?"

They sed, "Shore, if'n y'all want to."

They put the target 20 feet out. But Red sed, "Make it 30 yards."

So they moved the target, and the instructor sed, "Shoot when
y'all're ready."

The instructor sed, "Who taught y'all how to shoot like that?"

Red sed, "My dad and my grandpa, John Fussell and Red Fussell."
He went on to tell 'im the story of how 'is grandpa tracked and kilt 4
men that kilt 'is own dad when he were jist 16 years old.

The class started on Monday. It lasted 8 weeks, and like he were told,
'bout half the class flunked out. Red wrote 'is grandma jist 'bout very
day. If'n 'is mama wanted to know what were goin' on, she were gonna
have to ask 'is grandma. Grandma Red looked for mail every day.

Red were #1 in 'is class and they asked 'im what he'd like to do.

He told 'is boss, "I'd like to work with a ranch." They had to work
with someone for 'bout 2 months, but he told 'is boss he'd done it afore,
and didn't need the trainin'. But they sent 'im to one of the biggest
ranches in Texas, Scott Ranch. When he got there, it were real hard to
tell how big it were, and they was thorns on every bush.

Scott Ranch

Chapter 48

Young Red learnt real fast that the cows knowed where the water hole were. The ranch foreman didn't think much of 'im. He sed he were dumb and that he wouldn't last long. Red didn't know it, but nobody lasted there very long. The man were real hard on most of the men.

The ranch had been losin' calves, and it'd been goin' on quite a few years. Red asked everybody, but it seemed nobody knowed nothin' about it. Red started watchin' the trucks that come in and left. He 'membered a time 'is grandpa caught them men stealin' calves by puttin' 'em in drums.

They were a big ole truck. It hauled jist 'bout everythin', oil, gas, water. Then he watched the foreman. Every Friday he'd leave for 5-6 hours. Red followed 'im to high country one Friday. He walked so the foreman wouldn't know he were there. Shore 'nuff, they was loadin' calves into drums.

Young Red eased back out, but he had the tag number of the truck. He called 'is boss and told 'im he needed help; but he didn't tell 'im what, in case he were part of it. But when he sed he needed help, they was 'bout 7 rangers there in 'bout 1 hour. Red told 'em what he seen. His boss thought Red were wrong, and he also called another man over. He didn't know it neither. They eased 'round to where they was loadin' the calves and seen 'em give the calves a shot, so they didn't make no noise.

They handed Red a loudspeaker and told 'im what to do. So Red sed into the speaker, "They's no need to run. All the roads is blocked." But Red noticed 'is boss done left. He got on the radio and asked where he were, but he didn't answer. So Red called the big boss and told 'im. He sed they had 'im and would bring 'im back. They had the ranch foreman. The boss told Red the foreman were fired.

Red jist smiled. He tried one of 'is grandpa's tricks. He asked to speak to one of the truck drivers. The driver looked scared, but Red told 'im if'n he told 'im what they did with the calves, he'd try to help 'im.

So Red got ahold of the big boss and told 'im what he'd done. He asked what he needed to do next. The big boss sed they hada put the calves where nobody would know. And to tell all the rangers to keep their mouths shut. The big boss sed he'd give the truck driver a deal, but he must tell everythin'.

They asked the driver where he took the calves. But the driver sed, "I can't tell y'all."

So Red sed, "Well, put 'im over with the foreman and the rest of the crooks."

The driver sed, "I ain't gonna help no crook that won't help me. The big boss will kill me."

Red sed, "The boss don't think y'all told me; he thinks the foreman did. But the foreman will soon be in jail and can't hurt y'all."

The driver sed, "But he has friends that might."

Red sed, "We'll put y'all in a safe place. But if'n y'all won't help us, y'all will go with them, and we'll tell 'em y'all told us."

So the driver told us. Then 4 rangers put on work clothes to look like cowboys. They took the calves out and hid them in a separate field. They bugged the truck and followed it to a big barn. The driver drove in and they closed the door. Red and the other rangers went through the back door. They was 4 people inside, but they didn't give no trouble. Red asked what they do with the calves, but they sed, "We ain't a gonna tell y'all."

Red sed, "Jist so y'all know, they hang cow thieves."

One of the men looked at Red with tears in 'is eyes and sed, "This here is jist a job for me. I didn't know they stole them calves."

Then they all decided they needed to tell where the calves was goin'. They sed they was goin' to Florida to Arcadia to the R.L. Carloup Ranch. It were one of the biggest ranches in Florida.

It were hard for young Red to believe that. He'd been to that ranch afore. He thought, I bet 'is boy's in the business of stealin' calves.

The rangers hauled them off to jail while they checked their story out. Young Red caught a ride to the airport and flew to Tampa. He called 'is dad to pick 'im up. He really wanted to talk with 'is grandpa 'bout the calf thiefs, and he wanted to see Grandma Red. He told 'is dad he had a free day.

So John picked 'im up at the Tampa Airport and took 'im to Dade City to see Grandma Red. When he got there he walked in to where she were sewin' and tried to set on her lap, as big as he were. She grabbed 'im, and then she cried. Red shore loved 'is Grandma Red.

Then young Red went to see 'is mama. Carla shore were glad to see 'im. They's jist no place like home.

He needed to go see 'is grandpa. So John took 'im to see Grandpa. When he walked up on the porch, I come out. Young Red told me how they caught the calf thieves, jist like I had done. He went on to tell me the thieves sed they take 'em to R.L. Carloup Ranch in South Florida. I looked at young Red real hard. I sed, "I know R.L. I don't think they would do nothin' like that."

It were gittin' late, so young Red sed, "I love y'all, Grandpa; I gotta go." He left for the airport to be picked up by the rangers. The truck would be in Arcadia the next day. He met 4 rangers at the airport and they picked up a car from the FBI. They loaned them some extra guns.

The next day they left for Arcadia, but when they got there, there weren't no truck. They went to the ranch, but nobody showed up. They waited till the next day and still no truck. Finally they sed, "I think we've been set up."

Red called the main office and they told 'im that the truck had burned on the highway, and the driver couldn't be found. So Red sed he would go inside the R.L. Carloup Ranch and look for the calves. They sed that would be fine.

Red couldn't find nothin' wrong. He talked to the son on the ranch and he told 'em he thought they'd been sent on a wild goose chase.

So Red called the office again. He wanted to talk with the 4 men that sent 'im to R.L. Carloup Ranch.

His boss sed, "Somebody kilt 'em."

Red thought, *This here's bigger than I thought it were.* He flew back to Texas late that night, but got a few hours of sleep on the plane. When he got to the ranch, he were told the ranch hands done left.

Red sed, "Then, we need to find 'em."

He asked everybody 'round the ranch, but nobody knowed nothin'. Then he thought, *If'n I could go see the ranch foreman in jail, I might git 'im to talk.*

So young Red went to the jail and got to talk to the foreman in a room. He told the foreman that 4 men had been kilt, and he may be charged for their deaths. He might even git the electric chair.

Well, the foreman changed right away. He sed, "If'n I tell y'all who's in charge, will y'all help me?"

Red sed, "If'n y'all turn in state's evidence, I'll help y'all."

The foreman sed, "Y'all need to look at the head bookkeeper, and check 'is personal bank account. He has a ranch in New Mexico, and that's where them calves is goin'. Y'all should check that ranch. Some of the calves will have the Scott Ranch mark in their ear."

Red had been on this job for 'bout 1 year and 7 months. The big boss at the ranch told 'im that the head bookkeeper sed they was spendin' way too much money on this case. So Red called 'is big boss and told 'im he needed to see 'im.

He left for Houston on Monday. When he got there 'is boss told 'im they was gonna stop lookin', that the calf stealin' had stopped. But Red told 'im what he learned 'bout the bookkeeper.

His boss sed, "That's why he wanted us to stop."

He sed, "Make like we's gonna stop, and I'll send a letter to the bookkeeper to ask 'im what date we should stop, so it'll be in writin'. I'll have the FBI check all 'is holdin's, how much money he has, and where in New Mexico he goes. I think we're on the right track."

In 'bout a month they had all the evidence they needed. The bookkeeper hadn't paid taxes on hardly no extra money he made. They could get 'im on that alone, but they wanted to git 'im on calf stealin', too.

Young Red asked the Ranger Captain if'n they could raid the camp in New Mexico. The Captain sed, "If'n y'all think y'all'll find anythin'."

Red sed, "Let's do it."

Red knowed 'bout 12 rangers he trusted. So the Captain called them in. Red told 'em what happened, and that they was gonna raid the bookkeeper's ranch in New Mexico. He sed, "We leave in 'bout an hour. We've told the girl in the office we will be gone for 'bout a week. We don't want no leaks. If'n anyone leaks any information he will go to jail. Does everyone understand?"

They left in a bus, but as they left Red had a feelin' somethin' warn't right and told the Captain. He sed, "I think they've been tipped off. One of this bunch has tipped 'em off this time. We'll make them all take a lie dector test." They took the bus to the next town and stopped at the local police department to use their equipment.

They lined the rangers up to take the test, and found the guilty one. It were Ralph. The Captain sed, "Ralph were with us for 20 years."

Red sed, "Can I test 'im?" Red looked 'im in the eyes and sed, "Why did y'all call the ranch and tell 'em we was comin'?"

Ralph jist looked at 'im. He'd made a big mistake.

Red sed, "What did y'all tell them?"

Ralph sed, "I told 'em to hide them calves where no one would find them."

Sed, "Where'd they hide 'em?"

He sed, "If'n I tell y'all, no tellin' what they'll do to my family."

Red sed, "What do they have on y'all?"

Ralph started to cry. "It were jist easy money ."

Red talked to the Captain and asked 'im to call the FBI and tell them the rangers we was still goin' to New Mexico. He called, and they caught a plane to New Mexico at a small airport, all except the Captain and Ralph.

The FBI arranged for a bus to meet the rangers. They laid on the bus floor as they drove through the gate up to the house. It were 'bout 10:30 at night. Then they woke everybody up.

They lined up all the cow hands and told 'em that they was goin' to check the calves the next day. Then they posted rangers outside to catch anyone that tried to move the calves in the night.

The next mornin', they found the Scott Ranch mark in the calves's ears. Red didn't think they even knowed about the ear mark. They questioned the ranch foreman there in New Mexico and he sed, "Mr. Big were not the bookkeeper. Mr. Big were a Texas Ranger."

Red asked, "Is 'is name, Ralph?"

He sed, "It shore is."

Red called the Captain and told 'im what the foreman told them. In 'bout 6 months, Ralph and most of the ranch hands was in jail.

The Call from Home

Chapter 49

Young Red got a call from home. It were Grandma Red. She told 'im 'is dad warn't doin' very good, and he needed help to run the ranch. She sed 'is grandpa had been real sick, too.

Red seen the Ranger Captain, and told 'im he needed to go home. The Captain sed, "Y'all should go now; but if'n y'all wanna come back, we'll take y'all."

Red went to see Scott, the ranch owner to tell 'im he were goin' home. The owner agreed he should go.

Red loaded 'is truck and had to git a trailer to put all 'is stuff in. He had a secret to tell Grandma Red; he done got married to the ranch owner's daughter, Samantha, a month afore. They left Texas and drove through the night. They got to Dade City 'bout 5:30 in the afternoon, and drove up to Grandma Red's house. He blowed the horn. Out come Grandma Red. She grabbed 'im and didn't want to turn 'im loose.

She seen a girl gittin' out of 'is truck. Red sed, "Grandma Red, this here's my wife. Her name is Samantha, but I call 'er Sam for short." His grandma on the Fussell side were named Sam, too.

Grandma Red sed, "Have y'all seen y'all's mama yet?"

He sed, "No. We're headed there now. I wanted to stop here first."

They drove on to Red's parents' house, 'bout a mile down the road.

Red seen the bell. He jist had to stop and ring it, 2 longs and 1 short. Patty were visitin' Mama and come runnin' out and hugged 'im. He told 'is wife, "This here's my sister. But watch out, 'cause she bites." They all laughed. And 'is mama run out of the house and grabbed 'im. Then she seen the girl. Carla walked over and told Sam that 'er name were Carla.

Red told 'is mama that Sam were 'is wife, and 'er name were really Samantha; but he called 'er Sam, for short.

Carla sed, "You know your dad's not doin' well. I shore am glad y'all're both here. How long can y'all stay?"

Red looked at 'er and sed, "As long as y'all need me."

They was tired and needed a bath and some sleep, but went to 'is parents' bedroom to see young Red's dad first. He knocked and opened the door. His dad did look bad. He were havin' trouble with 'is heart. Red told 'im that the girl with 'im were 'is wife. He sed, "I'm in love with 'er jist like y'all was with my mama. Her name is Samatha, but I call her Sam.

John sed, "I know somebody that shore is gonna like y'all."

Red told 'is dad they was tired and needed a bath. So they took a bath and went to bed. The next mornin' Carla had breakfast cooked. She asked Sam what she liked, but Sam sed she'd eat whatever Carla cooked.

Grandma Red walked in the house and went straight to the dinin' room, got 'er a plate and set down next to Red. She sed, "I'm so glad y'all're here." Red could see tears in 'er eyes and she sed, "It 'bout broke my heart when y'all went to Texas. I was so mad at y'all and I was mad at y'all's Mama for lettin' y'all go."

Grandma Red sed, "Red, I'm gonna move in with Barbara, and y'all and Sam can have my house."

Sam sed, "We don't want to take y'all's house."

Grandma sed, "But I want y'all to have it, so y'all'll be close by. I ain't a gonna let y'all git away from me again."

Young Red told 'is dad he wanted to go see 'is grandpa, and thought he and Sam would ride over to Bill's ranch. John told 'im to go ahead.

Grandma told them she would have their stuff moved inside whilst they was gone.

It looked like it might rain. Red and Sam left to go to Bill's ranch. It took them a little over an hour to git there. He needed to put 'is pistols on. Sam asked why he were wearin' them, and he sed, "Cause my grandpa give 'em to me."

When they got there, Kyle walked out of the house. He walked up to the truck. He was as tough as any cowboy in the woods. Kyle sed, "Grandpa's on the porch. He sets there every day, and all he wants is to be with Sam."

Young Red told Kyle this were 'is wife, Samantha, but he called 'er Sam. You shoulda saw the look on Kyle's face and he sed, "I know somebody that shore is gonna like 'er."

Red hadn't told 'er 'bout Grandpa's Sam, so he told 'er now. She sed, "I shore hope he likes me."

They walked in the house with Kyle. Sarah seen young Red, and Red sed, "This here's my wife Samantha, but I call her Sam, for short."

Sarah smiled and sed, "I know somebody that's shore gonna like her." Sarah give them a cup of coffee, and told 'em to take it on the porch where Red were settin'.

Sam sed, "Grandpa, here's your coffee."

I looked at 'er and were tryin' to figure out jist who she were. And then my grandson, young Red, grabbed 'is pistols and shot the iron pipe. Then I knowed who it were.

I sed, "Boy, y'all scared me to death." They all laughed. I sed, "I'm shore glad y'all is home, but who's the purty girl there?"

Young Red put 'is arm 'round 'er and sed, "This here's my wife."

I sed, "Congratulations! What's 'er name?"

Young Red sed, "Sam."

I sed, "Now, don't kid with me."

Young Red sed, "I'm not. Her real name is Samatha, but I call 'er Sam for short."

I sed, "That were my wife's name, too. I lost her a long time ago. I loved her so much, and each day I miss 'er more and more. The only way I'm gonna be happy is when I'm with 'er." I knowed I had tears in my eyes.

Sam leaned down and kissed me on the cheek. That shore made me feel good. Young Red could see a twinkle in my eyes."

I told Sam, "I shore hope y'all love my grandson jist like I loved my Sam."

Bill drove up and greeted us all, but sed he wanted to go take a bath. He'd been out with the cows, and it warn't a clean job. But afore he left to take 'is bath, young Red told 'is Uncle Bill that Sam were 'is wife."

Bill sed, "That were my mama's name."

Young Red told Bill that Sam's dad owned the biggest ranch in Texas. And sed, "She has 3 brothers and they run the ranch with 'bout 75 people. That's the ranch I worked for when I were in Texas."

Bill then left to clean up. Afore long he were back out with clean clothes on. He asked young Red what he were gonna do now, and young Red sed, "I guess I'm gonna run my dad's ranch."

Bill sed, "I'm the head of the Cattlemen Association. They need someone to stop the cow thieves around here. The state will pay y'all good money. They all heard what y'all done in Texas."

Finally, Red told Bill he would work for the state part time, but didn't want to work at it full time.

Bill sed, "My neighbor wants to find out what's goin' on."

Red told 'im to have the neighbor call 'im.

Bill sed he would, and for 'im to jist keep track of 'is hours for payment.

Red turned to Sam and sed, "Let's go to Homosassa. We can stop at the restaurant for a cup of coffee and walk down to the dock."

When they got to Homosassa, they looked out at the river, and young Red could see why 'is dad and 'is Uncle Bill and I loved this place. They got a cup or coffee and then he turned to Sam and sed, "We best be on our way." And they started to Dade City.

Red were drivin' a little fast and looked up. They were a red light flashin', so he stopped. The policeman walked up to the truck and sed, "If'n it ain't that red-headed boy from Dade City. Do y'all 'member me?"

Red sed, "No, can't place y'all."

He sed, "Y'all blacked both my eyes one time when I sed somethin' 'bout the way them girls lived, and y'all didn't like what I sed."

Red sed, "Oh, yes. Now I 'member."

The policeman sed, "I married 'er! And we still laugh 'bout it. Y'all was good to them girls, and I want to thank y'all for what y'all done. Sometime, when y'all git some time, let's go have lunch. Oh, and take it a little slower on the road." He got in 'is car and left.

James Carlton Fussell

Red and Sam looked at each other and they both laughed. Sam sed, "Did y'all like to fight?"

Red didn't answer. He jist laughed.

They got back to Dade City 'bout dark. They stopped at 'is mama's house first. She had supper cooked and they all et together. Then Red set in a chair and went to sleep. He were plumb tired.

When someone tried to wake 'im, he sed, "Jist let me be." When he woke up, the sun were up. Sam spent the night with Grandma Red.

The Hog Thief

Chapter 50

Young Red and Sam moved in to Grandma Red's house. 'Bout a week later, he got a call from Woody Wagner over on the Withlacoochee River. Somebody were cuttin' the tails and left ears off 'is hogs and lettin' 'em run loose in the swamp. He marked all 'is hogs, and when they had pigs, he marked them too.

Wagner had 2 boys that helped 'im run 'is saw mill. If'n somebody wanted to saw their trees, he cut them in halves. Then he got half the lumber. They stayed busy jist 'bout all the time. They owned a big tract of land on the river.

So Red took off to the river. He stopped by and seen Bill and told 'im what Mr. Woody sed 'bout them hogs over the phone. Bill's boys was standin' close by and they all laughed.

Kyle, one of the boys, sed, "Well, them pigs can't even wipe they's behinds with they's tails gone."

Kyle told Red he seen them hogs with the ear and tail gone. Red told them he had to go to the swamp. They sed it weren't far from Bill's house. Wagners was real good neighbors.

Red went to Woody's house 'bout noon. When he got out of 'is truck, Ken, one of Woody's boys, sed he shore liked Red's guns. Then he asked, "Can y'all shoot them?"

Young Red asked Woody if'n it were alright if'n he shot some

James Carlton Fussell

pine cones.

He sed, "Shore."

Red drawed both guns, fired 4 shots and 4 pine cones fell. Then the boy wanted to know where he learned how to shoot like that.

Red sed, "My grandpa taught me to shoot. His name's Red Fussell from over in Homosassa. He'd throw a rock in the air for me to shoot."

Then Red told Woody, "I can catch who's doin' it, but it may take some time. The cattlemen will pay for 4 days, but it may take longer. I could swap a day for lumber, if'n that's okay."

Woody sed, "I know the Fussell bunch. Y'all will be fair with me. Jist do it."

Red asked Ken if'n he wanted to help 'im and show 'im the lay of the land. So Ken saddled up 2 horses and they rode the edge of the swamp. Red noticed a dim trail and could tell somethin' had been walkin' on it. He asked Ken where the trail went, but he didn't know. So Red dropped it and thought he'd check it out later on 'is own.

They was lots of trails. He thought he'd look at all of 'em, but that one trail looked like somethin' a crook would use.

They rode for 'bout half a day, and then went back to the house. Red started to leave, but Woody stopped 'im. He sed, "Red, supper's ready, and my wife wants y'all to stay."

Red knowed he should git back home, but he stayed. It shore were a good supper. Arlene were a real good cook.

Well, it were gittin' dark, so he called Sam to tell 'er he wouldn't be home tonight. He were gonna catch the man that were cuttin' the one ear and tail off them hogs. Sam jist laughed and sed she would go to Carla's for the night.

After supper Red asked if'n he could use one of the horses. He didn't want no saddle and asked if'n the horse would come back home if'n he turned 'im loose.

Woody sed, "He would."

Red done got 'is gear out of the truck and the skeeter net. That shore would come in handy. He got the horse and took the bridle off and hid it in a tree. Then he eased down the trail. He jist felt they were someone else in the woods.

So he moved off the trail. A man walked right by 'im. Red knowed he probably lived in the swamp. He looked at 'is feet. He didn't have no shoes on. Lots of swamp people don't wear shoes. That's so they can slip through the woods.

Red started to follow 'im. Then the man stopped and were lookin' 'round like he knowed someone were on the trail. But Red knowed the man would stay on the trail, or at least he hoped he would. They went 'bout 2 miles and then the man stopped. There were 'is hog trap. He had a little chute so's he could cut the ears off.

Red walked up to 'im and sed, "I'm the law. Don't try to run. Put y'all's hands behind y'all's back."

Then Red built a fire so he could see who the man were. The man turned 'round and looked Red in the face. He sed, "My name's Will. I lived here in these woods all my life."

Red asked, "Why do y'all cut the tails and ears off'n the hogs? Y'all know they can put y'all in jail for that."

Will sed, "They ain't much to eat out here no more, and 'bout all I can buy is rice. Them ears and tail, they gonna throw away anyhow, so I didn't think they'd mind if'n I et 'em."

Then he wanted to know who Red were. Red told 'im that he worked for the government and that 'is dad's name were John Fussell, and 'is grandpa's name were Red Fussell from Homosassa.

Will sed, "I worked for 'im on 'is boat."

Red took the handcuffs off 'im. He didn't think Will'd need them. Red told 'im to let the hog out of the pen.

Will sed, "Okay, but some of them hogs is real bad."

Red built a bigger fire to keep them skeeters off. He'd brought some food from Arlene's table' cause he never knowed how long he'd be gone. Red handed Will 'is canteen and sed, "Git y'all'self a drink of water."

Will sed, 'If'n I take a drink, y'all won't drink after me."

Red sed, "Oh, yes, I will."

Red give 'im part of the food he had, and they set and talked 'bout some of the thangs he done. Will didn't know how old he were, but thought he were 'bout 88. Red asked 'im where he lived.

Will sed, "It's an ole house in the edge of the swamp. It were 'bout the only place I could stay for nothin.'"

Red thought, *What would Grandpa do if'n he were here? I wanna let 'im go, but he broke the law.*

James Carlton Fussell

They set by the fire all night. When daylight started to break, Red told 'im it were time for them to go.

They started out of the swamp. Will stopped. So Red stopped. Will sed, "They's somethin' in front of us."

Red looked, but didn't see nothin'. Then it moved. It were a big ole bore hog with one ear missin' and 'is tail were gone. Red laughed. Will looked at Red and sed, "He shore tasted good." And they both laughed.

When they got to the place where Red put the bridle, he couldn't find it. Will sed he hid it. So he walked out in the woods and brought it back.

They put away the horse and walked up to Woody's house. Ken seen 'em comin' and wanted to know if'n the man were the one that cut the ears and tails off 'em hogs. But Red told Ken to git 'is dad.

Woody come outside and Red sed, "I need to talk to y'all 'bout this." Woody and Red walked behind the house, and Red told 'im why the man done what he done.

Red sed, "I can take 'im to jail, but I don't wanna do that. He jist didn't have nothin' to et, and folks throw them ears and tails away, anyhow."

Woody looked at Red and smiled. Woody sed, "I have that ole house by the barn. We can fix it up so he can live there. I can let 'im take care of the chicken feedin' and waterin' and pickin' up the eggs."

So Woody called to 'is sons, Ken and Bert, and sed, "Y'all boys go clean that ole house, so Will can live in it."

Ken sed, "I ain't gonna clean it. He stinks!"

Red seen Woody's face and knowed somethin' was fixin' to happen. Then Woody sed, "Then we'll jist move Will into your bedroom."

Red told Woody he would pay 'is rent. Woody jist smiled and sed, "Don't worry 'bout what it costs. I'll take care of it." Then Woody told Red, "If'n you need some lumber, jist let me know. I'll give y'all some."

Red sed he needed to be on 'is way. He wanted to git home afore dark, but he needed to talk with Will first. Red went to the front of the house. Will were standin' there. He warn't shore he warn't goin' to jail. But Red walked up and hugged 'im and told 'im, "This is y'all's lucky day!"

Red seen Ken's face and knowed he warn't happy to have Will 'round. Woody seen it, too. Woody would make Ken take Will's lunch to 'im every day.

At first Ken didn't wanna do it, but afore long Woody noticed he stayed out there more and more. One day Woody were lookin' for 'is forge and anvil. They was gone. He asked Ken if'n he knowed where they was, and Ken sed he took them down to Will's house.

Them boys done worked hard and cleaned Will's house purty good. At night after Bert went to bed, Ken would go down to Will's house. Will were teachin' 'im how to blacksmith. They done made a knife, and they was workin' on somethin' else, but Ken wouldn't say what it were. Anytime someone come 'round, Ken would hide it.

Sometimes Ken would spend the night with Will, and then Bert would kid 'im 'bout it. Bert sed, "You smell like Will!" They was fixin' to fight, but Woody put a stop to it.

They was a fair in Inverness and Ken wanted to go. He had somethin' he wanted to sell. Woody asked what it were, but Ken wouldn't tell. Finally, Woody sed he'd take 'im to the fair.

Ken had a big box, but wouldn't let Woody look in it. When he opened the box up in Inverness, they was the best lookin' spurs Woody ever seen.

Ken asked Woody if'n 10 dollars was too much to ask for 'em. But Woody sed, "No. Y'all will sell every one of 'em for that!" They had 20 that they done made. Ken called 'em, "Will Spurs."

A cowboy from down in Arcadia stopped to look at 'em. He sed, "How much?"

Ken told 'im, "10 dollars each."

He picked up every one of 'em, and then he sed, "I'll take 'em all."

Ken never added up that much money afore. Half were 'is money and half were Will's. Then the man told 'im, "If'n y'all git silver dollars and make 'em spurs, they'll sell even better." So Ken took 20 dollars and got 20 silver dollars. He were real happy with what 'im and Will had done.

When he got back home, he gave 'is money to Will, but Will didn't wanna take it. Then Ken showed 'im the silver dollars and Will sed, "I wanna buy one of 'em silver dollars." Ken tried to give it to 'im, but Will wouldn't take it.

Ken went to work on a new spur. When he were done, it were silver inlaid, the best he ever seen. He asked Woody to take 'im to Dade City.

He wanted to git Will somethin' for Christmas.

Ken told Will he were goin' to Dade City and would be gone all day, but afore he left he picked up an ole pair of Will's pants and a shirt.

They went to see John Fussell, and then on to see Sandy. Ken told 'er he needed a pair of them good pants and a shirt. Sandy sed, "Y'all know what it costs?"

Ken sed, "How much?"

But 'bout then young Red walked in. Ken handed 'im a bag and when he opened it, there was the silver spurs Will done made for 'im.

Sandy looked at Ken and then Red. Red shook 'is head at 'er. So she sed, "I'll let y'all know when I git 'em done."

John walked in and Red showed 'im them silver spurs. John sed, "I want a set of 'em."

Ken told 'em he needed to git some more silver dollars. Red told John he'd be back and he wouldn't be gone long. He were back in jist a short time. He had 50 silver dollars and sed he wanted 2 pair.

Ken sed, "If'n I pay for the clothes I can't pay for the silver dollars."

So John sed, "That's for 2 spurs."

Then John told Sandy to make the boy a pair of them ridin' pants and a shirt and he would pay for it. Ken didn't know why John were payin' for 'is pants and shirt, but then John told him somethin' a man named, Ray, sed, "Never be greedy". He told Ken to always remember that.

John told Ken, "Red told me y'all didn't want Will at y'all's house. But now, y'all wouldn't want 'im to leave. Right?"

Ken sed, "That's right. Will taught me everythin'."

A couple of weeks later, John come by to see Bill and then he went to Woody's. He called Ken to come out. He had somethin' for 'im. Ken asked John what he owed for the clothes. But John sed, "My wife wants some silver spurs."

Ken sed, "I'll be right back." He had 'bout 10 pair made up and he handed a set to John. Then John gave 'im a package, but sed, "Don't open it till I leave."

Ken watched John leave and wished he would hurry up so he could look inside the package. By the time John were out of sight, Ken were almost shakin' with excitment. He opened the package with 'is mama standin' there watchin'. It were a white shirt with ruffles and a bow tie.

Ken put it all on and went down to show Will.

Will sed, "Lord 'o mercy! Y'all shore look dressed up."

Ken went back to the house, and 'is mama asked if'n he were gonna give Will 'is clothes. But Ken sed, "Not till Christmas."

The next weekend on Saturday they went to Inverness. Ken and Bert was walkin' the streets. Ken paid to see the picture show and stopped to look at a man drawin' a picture of a woman. He'd draw 'er and then he'd paint 'er. Ken walked in and asked how much did it cost, and he sed, "5 dollars."

Well, Ken seen a man pay 'im 4 dollars, so he sed, "I'll give y'all 4 dollars jist like 'im."

The man sed, "Ok."

Ken went and got Will and told 'im to look in the window at what they do. He went in and told the man that this were the man he wanted in the drawin' and paintin'. But when the artist seen he were a black man, he sed, "Y'all really want me to paint 'im?"

Ken sed, 'Yes." He give 'im 4 dollars, and Will walked off.

Then Ken told the man he really wanted the man to draw a pig with Will cuttin' 'is left ear off, and could he do that?

He sed, "I'm not shore I can do it." So Ken give 'im one more dollar and he sed he could do it.

He sed he would have it did in a week. Ken told 'im he weren't plannin' to be back in town in a week, but he'd try.

The next Saturday they went back to town. Ken really wanted that picture. He hadn't told no one about it. But when they got to town, he seen the store were closed. He thought shore he'd done lost 'is 5 dollars, and 'is heart were jist broken. He started to walk off, but then he seen the picture next door. He went inside and asked if'n that were 'is picture. The man give it to 'im. It looked jist like Will.

Ken got 'im a paper bag and put Will's picture in the bag. Bert wanted to know what were in it, but Ken wouldn't tell 'im. When he got home he put it under the bed.

It were now December and Christmas would soon be there. Will told Ken he never ever got a Christmas present afore. Ken thought, *He's in for a big surprise this time!*

Woody told them they was gonna have a big Christmas tree this year. They cut a tree and put some sweetgum balls on it. Arlene

James Carlton Fussell

punched a hole in raw eggs and blew out the yokes, cleaned the empty egg shells, and hung 'em on the tree.

Sweetgum Balls

Ken asked 'is dad, "Could Will come to the Christmas party?" Woody jist looked at 'im and then he sed, "For someone who didn't want Will here, y'all shore changed. I don't see why not, but he'll need to eat in the kitchen."

Ken sed, "Can I eat with 'im?"

Arlene were cookin' Christmas dinner and they had a bunch of people comin'. Ken were gonna eat with Will in the kitchen. Bert could eat where he wanted to. Ken told Will he had to take a bath first, so while Will were takin' a bath in the river, he stole 'is clothes and left the new pants and shirt for 'im to put on.

When Will walked up to the house, he shore looked good. He walked up to Ken, and Ken seen tears in 'is eyes. He sed, "Ken, this is the best Christmas I ever had in my life."

Whilst Will were takin' a bath, Ken put the picture in 'is house. He wished he could be there when Will seen it.

Sarah fixed a couple of plates and the 2 of them et in the kitchen. Ken give Bert one of 'em silver spurs with 'is name on it. And he give 'is dad silver spurs with 'is name on it. Will done it for 'im. Ken often wondered what it woulda been like if'n Will hadn't a been there. Ken give 'is mama the last 5 dollars he had so she could get what she wanted. This shore were a nice Christmas.

Then Will handed Ken a box. Inside were a horse with 'im on it. Ken grabbed 'im and hugged 'im. Ken done seen young Red Fussell grab 'im and hug 'im, and couldn't understand it then. But he did now.

Will died in March. It 'bout broke Ken's heart. He hated he died, but knowed he were old. Woody made a casket. Ken helped dig the hole and they put up a fence around the grave.

Woody walked in Will's house and seen the picture on the wall. He jist laughed. They shore was glad to have Will 'round. He done took care of the chickens till the day he died.

Years passed and Woody were old. Bert, he become a Baptist preacher in Lakeland. Ken is still in the lumber business and were into big lumber buyin' in the thousands. Will's picture were hangin' there, and a man asked who it were. Ken sed, "That's the best friend I ever had."

The picture were of Will cuttin' the pig's ear off, and it looked jist like 'im.

Later whilst Ken were out west at a cattlemen's auction, they was sellin' all kinds of stuff. They brought out a pair of silver spurs. He knowed who made them. He bid 50 dollars, but the man next to 'im bid 500 dollars. Ken knowed he didn't need them.

Then when the man paid for them he sed, "Hey, y'all made them spurs didn't y'all?

Ken sed, "Yes."

The man jist give the spurs to 'im.

The Last of the Legend

Chapter 51

Bill called and told Carla their dad died while settin' on the porch. He sed he had a smile on 'is face 'cause now he were with their mom.

Carla rung the bell 2 short and 1 long and done it again. John knowed somethin' were wrong, so he rushed to the house. Carla told John 'is dad done died sittin' on Bill's porch.

John took a quick bath and left for Bill's. He told Carla to stay home and he would call with what they needed to do.

He got to Bill's. They'd done picked up the body and would embalm 'im, so the body wouldn't smell real quick.

Bill sed, "He's happy now. He's with our mom."

John told Bill he would go get the casket in Homosassa that their dad wanted to be buried in. It were jist like Sam's.

John picked up the casket at the fish house. Then he went down on the dock and asked one of the fishermen if'n he could rent one of 'is boats. The man looked at John and sed, "Y'all's dad died?"

John sed, "Yes."

The fisherman sed, "He bought that boat for me. I never paid all it back. He wouldn't take it. Y'all can have it any time. I'll clean it up."

Then John sed, "They's no need to clean it up."

John left Homosassa and headed to Inverness to the funeral home.

When he got there Bill were there with a paper bag. They took the casket inside. The funeral director looked at it and sed, "I know y'all can buy a better casket than that."

Bill told 'im, "This is what he wanted."

The funeral director sed, "Where will he be buried?"

Bill sed, "The funeral will be in Homosassa."

He handed the funeral director the paper bag. It had that table cloth in it. The director looked at Bill and then he sed, "He were a strange man. He'd help anybody down on 'is luck." A tear come to 'is eye. "He helped me one time. I wanted to go to embalmin' school and he loaned me the money. When I tried to pay 'im back he sed, "Jist embalm me when I die."

Bill handed 'im the shoe and told 'im to put it in the casket. The director knowed that shoe musta meant somethin' in Red's life, but didn't wanna ask.

Carla called Lewis' family. She sed she would let 'em know when the funeral would be. She called 'er sister, Judy, in Okahumpka. Young Red shore were upset when he heard. Grandma Red told 'im, "He's with Sam now, so be happy for 'im."

News traveled fast. When John were in Homosassa, he looked at the church. It didn't need paintin'. John told Sam's sister, Sally, that 'is dad died, and he would let 'er know when the funeral would be.

Bill and John got together and sed the funeral would be at 10 in the mornin' on Friday in Homosassa. John called Sally, and told her to tell everybody in Homosassa.

Friday come 'round real quick. Homosassa were full of people gathered for the funeral.

When Bill drove up, he parked in the middle of the road. There were no way the church would hold them all, so jist the family went to the church. John already dug the grave. He took young Red to help 'im. They got the metal box that Red made for the wood casket, jist like Sam's.

"Bout 9:45 they went inside the church. The preacher sed what he thought were the right thang to say, and the service were over. They placed Red in the metal box, made it watertight and took it to the shrimp boat. They were a man standin' there with tears in 'is eyes. It were Earl, the tax man. John spoke to 'im and they loaded the casket into the boat.

The boat owner asked if'n they would need help, but John told 'im they could handle it. Then John 'membered he hadn't put that gold coin in 'is hand, but Bill told 'im he done it. John shore were glad.

They went through Hell's Gate, left, 2 rights, 2 lefts, right, and headed to the Gulf. Then turned left and pulled up. They hooked the metal box to the boom, loaded it in the hole, filled the hole with dirt and brush so no one could tell where they buried 'im.

When they put the metal box in the hole, the box made a funny noise, or did they jist want it to?

More Tales
from the Withlacoochee River

Woodson Island

This island is on the Withlacoochee River. It's 'bout 10 acres with most good farmland and some good timber. It were homesteaded by Frank Woodson's grandparents 'bout 1914, and they lived there till they died.

They found Woodson and 'is wife, shot, and floatin' in the river. They sed they knowed who shot 'em, but couldn't prove it. They sed ole man Henley, or one of 'is boys, done it.

Henley told everybody he paid Mr. Woodson for the land, but jist didn't git a bill of sale. And it were 'is! Henley didn't know Mr. Woodson's grandson, Frank and 'is wife, Martha, was comin' to git 'is grandad's land, and he had the legal deed.

Frank got there on a Friday. He borrowed a boat from Jerry. Jerry told 'im to jist keep it 'cause he never used it. Frank oared it out to the house. The house needed lots of work, but Frank could do the work. His grandfather had a small saw mill. It were wind-driven, so when the wind blowed, he could saw timber.

They brought their dog with them. He were a gentle dog all day, but when it'd git dark, he'd git bad. He didn't jist bark. He bit. He'd sneak up on what he were gonna bite, bite them, then he'd run.

They spent the first night burnin' rags to git rid of them skeeters, snakes and roaches. They cleaned 'round the house the best they could. That afternoon, ole man Henley come by. He told Frank he bought this place, but didn't git no bill of sale. But he knowed it were 'is and he wanted 'em to leave.

Frank looked at 'im and sed, "I have the legal deed that says it's mine, and I'm a gonna keep it." Henley had two boys with 'im and sed, "These here boys could put a good whippin' on y'all, if'n y'all don't git off my land.

Martha heard what were goin' on. She were still in the house, but she had the rifle filled with shells. Them boys started toward Frank, and Martha put a round on one of them boy's shoes, jist in front of 'is toe. The boys stopped. Frank told Henley, "The next shot will be 'is ear."

They didn't run to their boat, but they didn't lose no time gittin' there neither. Now that ole dog were layin' under the porch. He were jist lookin' like nothin' were happenin'.

Frank walked back to the house and told Martha, "We're gonna have trouble with them." That night 'bout 2 o'clock, they heard somebody scream like he'd been shot.

It were a dark night, and Frank didn't know the lay of the land yet, so he didn't go out there.

Martha sed, "Where's the dog?"

Frank sed, "He's where that feller hollered. They was some runnin' through the woods and someone were a-hollerin'. I think that dog done bit 'im."

When it got daylight, they et grits and eggs and had some coffee that Frank's grandma left.

He walked down to the boat landin'. They was blood all over the ground, and they laid a rifle on the ground. He jist pitched it in the river and sed to himself, "I bet they don't want no more of that dog!"

Frank told Martha, "We need to go to Inverness to check on the bank and Grandpa's land grant."

They left the dog in charge. He stayed under the house where it were cool. They had their horses over at Mr. Wagner's place till they settled in.

They went to the land office and was told, "Yes, the land belonged to them." They checked with the bank, and they had more money than they thought they had. They was rich. His grandpa done left it all to Frank, and he left a note to watch out for Mr. Henley. Sed he were a big crook.

James Carlton Fussell

They stopped at the sheriff's office and told 'im what happened. The sheriff sed, "Them boys got chewed up bad by a panther last night. One of the boy's face is shore a mess. They sed they was in the river swamp."

Frank sed, "No, they met our dog out at our place."

Martha bought sugar, salt, a bunch of canned goods, flour, all kinds of spices and some gulf spray with a pump sprayer to spray for skeeters. Then they stopped at the gun shop and bought 4 guns. One were a 45-70. And they got plenty of bullets.

The feller at the gun shop told 'em to be careful. "That bunch is a bad bunch," he sed.

When they got back to the house, somebody done shot the side of the house. Frank eased inside, but they weren't no damage there. He called the dog. He come out. He'd been shot, but not bad.

That day Frank put up jist a one strand of bobwire, and stretched it tight as he could git it from one tree to 'nother. He put it 'bout neck high so anyone runnin' through there would git caught on the bobwire. It'd knock 'im clear off 'is feet.

When he were in Inverness he bought some skeeter net. He were gonna use it to go over their bed, but took that there net and made a blind out by the river. He thought he'd spend the night there in case they come back. He could hide under that net and keep the skeeters off.

He took the dog with 'im and put 'im under the skeeter net, too. He'd jist 'bout got to sleep when the dog moved. He seen 2 images easin' through the trees. The dog left afore Frank could catch 'im. Frank watched 'im.

The dog let one man go by, but he grabbed the other's hand. Frank could hear the bones jist a crackin'. The man screamed! Everybody on the island could hear 'im. The other one come back, raised 'is gun to shoot the dog, but Frank stopped 'im. He done shot 'is hand. He screamed and was bleedin' real good.

Frank walked out. Then he built a fire. He wrapped the man's hand and asked 'im what he were doin' there. He sed, "Mr. Henley done paid 'im to burn the house down."

Frank tied 'im to a tree and found the other one huddled on the ground behind a tree on the other side of the house. He tied 'im up over by the other one, and then sent Martha to Mr. Woody's house to git the sheriff. In 'bout an hour the sheriff got there. One of the men told the sheriff that Mr. Henley paid 'im to burn down the house there.

The sheriff told Frank that them 2 boys is known for lying 'bout everythin'. No court would even listen to them. He sed, "I know y'all're havin' trouble with Henley. He's bad to the bone. Y'all be careful when y'all go outside."

Frank put the dog inside the house till dark for the next 2-3 weeks. They had no trouble. Then late one night that dog done caught 'im somethin'. Frank thought, It's probably someone. Then he heard a shot. He thought, *They done kilt my dog.* Frank woke Martha to git 'er gun. Sed he were goin' outside to see if'n they'd kilt the dog.

Frank eased through the trees and shore 'nuff, they done kilt 'im. So he went down to the river and untied their boat, and give it a shove. The river would take it to the Gulf.

He were headin' back to the house when he seen the flash of light of a gun shot. Then he seen a man runnin' on fire. The man headed to the river and jumped in. He shoulda knowed better'n do that, cause a gator caught 'im real fast. Frank seen 'im go under and seen the blood. There weren't nothin' he could do. That boy were gone, and Frank didn't even know who he were.

He eased back to the house. He knocked 2 times and then 1 time. Martha knowed it were 'im so she opened the door. She told 'im, "He lit a cole oil bottle and I shot the bottle." She thought they were one more out there.

They waited until day light and looked, but couldn't find nobody. Frank walked to the landin'. There set one of Henley's sons. He were lookin' at the water and could see 'is brother's shirt with blood all over it. He done laid 'is gun down and sed, "Don't kill me."

Frank made 'im dig a grave for the dog, but he thought it were for 'im. Frank sent Martha to Mr. Woody's to git the sheriff again. He were there in jist a short time. The boy told the sheriff, "My dad told us to burn the house down, and to kill them inside like they did 'is grandpa, and to kill that dog."

The sheriff went to Mr. Henley's house. He come out with 'is gun, but the sheriff told 'im to put it down. He put the gun down and sed, "Is my boys dead?"

The sheriff sed, "The gator got one of them. The other one's in jail."

Then he put handcuffs on 'im.

He wanted to know what the charge were, and the sheriff sed, "Murder." They give 'is boy life in prison. They give 'im a rope.

Frank went on to raise 2 boys and 1 girl on that island.

The sheriff sed, "Jist 'member, when y'all try to take somethin' that don't belong to y'all, y'all might git somethin' y'all don't want."

Frank and Martha's girl married a preacher, one of their boys become a lawyer and the other boy become a teacher.

Frank and Martha lived out their life on the island. They died of old age. Frank sed, "They et so many of them turtles that when somethin' didn't go right, he'd jist try to pull 'is neck in."

The Juke Joint
on the Withlacoochee River

They was 2 people, Joe and Margaret, that come from up north somewhere. They was gonna fish and frog hunt to make a livin', not too far from Inverness along the Withlacoochee River. Little did they know it's hard work with very little money. They had 'nough money to jist git by.

They bought ole man Johnson's run-down ranch. Even 'is hogs was run down. Don't think Johnson told 'em the truth 'bout the ranch. They didn't look like people that would work hard, neither. They tried to make a go of it, but it didn't look good.

They were an ole black lady who lived in the chicken pen. It were jist a place to sleep.

Joe and Margaret took a likin' to 'er. They called 'er Marie. She weighed 'bout 400 pounds.

The ranch had a good chicken pen with a bunch of chickens. They sold some eggs and had 'bout 30 fryers. Marie told Margaret, "I could shore cook 'em chickens good."

Margaret told Joe to make a sign that sed, "Fried Chicken Lunch". "We gonna do lunch on Saturday."

So, come Saturday, Joe killed 3 chickens. They built a fire in the wood stove. Marie got the lard, then she mixed up somethin' special. Margaret didn't know what it were, but it looked like a mess. Marie baked some biskits and cooked some beans. They done put the sign up. Sed, "Fried Chicken Lunch for 1 dollar."

James Carlton Fussell

Joe sed, "That's too much."

Saturday they was ready.

The first man stopped. He sed, "That shore is high, but if'n it's good, it'll be worth it." He got a plate. He done et everythin' but the bones. He looked at Margaret and sed, "That there's the best chicken I ever et."

In 'bout an hour they was out of food and they'd made 9 dollars clear. Joe had to kill more chickens. They knowed they'd have more people stop.

All week long they was gittin' ready for Saturday. Joe killed 6 chickens and picked the feathers off. They baked the beans and put a piece of bacon in it. Marie shore were sweatin' when Saturday come 'round.

Margaret opened the door and there stood her first customer. He were there with 'is wife. He sed, "I'll have 2 of them chicken dinners."

Joe laughed. "They done et a lot of chicken, and they et all but the bones."

Then the man sed, "How much for the sauce?"

Margaret sed, "I'll have to let y'all know."

They was people standin' in line. They done et it all up, and Joe and Margaret, with Marie, made 18 dollars clear. That were almost a month's wages.

Then Marie told Margaret to git some ribs. She could cook them special.

Margaret asked how many she should git, but soon learned that Marie couldn't count. She shore could cook, though.

Marie told Joe how she wanted a hole dug. Then she built a big fire. Friday night they put an ole gate over it. Marie told Margaret what she wanted to make the sauce, but she told Margaret, "Don't sell the sauce. They'll have to come to us to git it to eat."

Marie mixed up a big bunch of sauce. Joe picked up the ribs Friday afternoon. They was was cheap. Margaret didn't know what Marie were gonna do, but Marie shore did. She put the ribs on the ole gate. She told Joe to turn the ribs every now and then. She made 'im a mop with a stick and a rag tied on it.

Joe told Margaret, "I shore hope that rag warn't 'er underwear!"

Joe jist done what Marie told 'im to do. He were turnin' and moppin' 'em ribs with the sauce. Marie told 'im when they was done. She told Joe to try a piece and to lock 'is teeth on it. It were real, real good.

He started to git 'im another piece, but Margaret sed, "No. We gotta clean 8 more chickens." They was 'bout to run out of chicken.

Then Marie told Joe to give everybody a rib that were in line. One man wanted a whole rib side. That sauce were what made it! They done made 20 dollars clear that day.

Margaret told Joe to go to Inverness and get a new stove. The one they had were 'bout wore out. So Joe took 15 dollars and a piece of rib with 'im. He found a good stove and give the man a piece of the rib. Then the man told Joe, "Cook me 10 slabs of ribs. I'll jist give y'all the stove, but I want the ribs on Friday afternoon."

Joe took the ribs in on Friday. They cost the man 2 dollars. He thought that were probably all the money that man had. Then Joe went to the butcher for more ribs and the butcher sed, "How many ribs will y'all need next week?"

Joe sed, "Get me 20."

The butcher sed, "Cook me 3 slabs, and I'll give y'all 20." That were a good deal. Then Joe left to go git the stuff for the sauce.

The man in the store told Joe, "Bring me a slab of ribs for this here bill."

They got to the place they didn't need to buy much no more. They jist swapped it for ribs. They done quit the fried chicken business. Everyone wanted ribs.

Joe called Ken Wagner, Woody's son, to build Marie a better house. He built 'er a real nice house. She cried when she moved in.

The money jist kept comin' in. The secret were in the sauce, and only Marie knowed how to make it.

Joe called Ken again to build them a big kitchen and dinin' room. Friday and Saturday the food business never quit. Margaret wanted a band to play while they et.

So Joe went to Inverness to look for a band. He stopped at the beer joint to git a beer. He asked the bartender if'n he knowed of a band. He told 'em they was 3 boys and an ole drunk. They both laughed.

Joe wanted their name and the bartender sed, "They work over at the sand mine." So Joe stopped by and seen one of the boys. He asked 'im if'n he would come over on Saturday night. He sed he would.

The week rolled 'round and Friday shore were busy. Then Saturday were busy till 'bout dark. The band showed up and Joe asked 'em how much they would charge. They sed, "Jist supper."

Joe sed, "We can do that." Joe made a stage and the band brought their stuff to play. He fed 'em first, but thought maybe he'd been better off if'n he'd paid them! One of them boys weren't big as nothin', but he et everythin' 'cept the table cloth! When they was through eatin', they started to play. Joe didn't know there was that many people in them woods. They done et 'bout everythin' Joe and Margaret had.

"Bout 10 o'clock he told the band to stop. They done a good job. He asked them how much did they owe them, but they jist sed, "Supper were real good." Joe give 'em 5 dollars, too. They was happy.

The next week, Marie cooked up a big pot of stew. It were good, too. She sed, "Sell it for 15 cents." The stew, plus the ribs they cooked, they was makin' big money.

Joe went back to Ken Wagner again and asked if'n he would build a dance floor and put screen up to keep them skeeters out. Ken worked all week. When he were done, Joe paid 'im. He done a good job. Joe told Margaret he were gonna charge 10 cents to dance, only Margaret didn't wanna charge. But come Saturday night, people didn't mind payin' at all.

Joe didn't like banks, so he bought a safe in Tampa, and hid it out by the outhouse, locked. And they started cookin' chicken again. Them people et 'bout anythin' Marie could cook. Joe told Marie to cook another pot of stew, but she sed she didn't have no more gopher. Joe jist laughed. Them people didn't know what they was eatin'. Marie shore were a good cook. Joe thought if'n she cooked rats they'd like them too. But she didn't.

This went on for 'bout 5 years. They made lots of money and tried to pay Marie, but she told 'em, "All I need are a place to stay."

On Monday a big storm were on the way, and they needed to bring everythin' they had inside. The wind done picked up. Joe went to Marie's to have 'er come the house with them, but Marie sed she were safe in 'er own house. Guess we all feel safe in our own house.

The wind picked up more. The trees was twistin'. The thunder and lightnin' was bad. Joe told Margaret it shore were a bad storm. They looked out their window and lightnin' struck Marie's house. It were on fire all over. Joe run to 'er house but seen he couldn't help. The wind blowed the fire to Joe and Margaret's house, too. Now everythin' were on fire. He run to 'is house. Margaret were outside. The house were built out of pine wood, so it burned like cole oil.

Joe and Margaret stood outside and jist watched it all burn up. The only thang that didn't burn up were the outhouse. It were all gone, but what they missed the most were Marie. She had been a blessin' to them.

Jist 'bout everybody come by. They didn't find much of Marie. They picked up what were left, dug a hole and Joe bought a box to put what they could find. They buried the box in the back yard and put 'er name on a stone marker, but didn't know 'er last name. So the marker jist sed, "Marie".

Margaret told Joe, "I can't stay here no more." They took the money out of their safe, saddled their horses, and rode off.

They told the land grant office to sell the land.

They rode to Tampa and no one heard nothin' 'bout them. Then one day, John Fussell went by a place to eat in Tampa. He looked up at a jar on the shelf and seen what it sed, "Best Meat Sauce in the world. Marie's Meat Sauce."

James Carlton Fussell

Hog Island

This here island were close to the Withlacoochee River, not too far from where Joe and Margaret's house burnt down. And it were 'bout as wild as it come. Most people didn't wanna git caught in that swamp at night.

They say they's a Green Man in that swamp. Some even say they seen 'im. He beats on trees with limbs and makes all kinds of noise. If'n y'all're campin', he puts y'all's fire out, cuts the rope on your tent and eats all y'all's food. He does everythin' to scare people. Some say he's crazy, and some knowed he were. They tried to trap 'im once, but he were too smart for that. A lady in Tampa sed he's got a still in them woods. So they was gonna send the revenuer out to catch 'im. They knowed Peg could smell 'im out.

Peg and Hal left Tampa on a Saturday. They had their tent and campin' gear. They took plenty of food 'cause Hal shore liked to eat. They got near Hog Island in a light rain, so they decided to sleep in their car till the rain let up. But it rained hard all night long. Everythin' were muddy.

When they git out of their car the next mornin', they looked at the car. All the tires was flat. Hal had a tire pump but that took 'bout all day. Peg set up the tent and opened the trunk to git the food. It were all gone. Somebody done stole it all! So they had to go back to Inverness to buy more food.

When they come back, they seen the tent were gone. Now they was gittin' mad. They went back to Inverness to git a good tent. When they git to their campin' site, the tent were there and the food were inside it. They were a fire goin'. They didn't know what were goin' on.

They cooked supper and were settin' by the fire. They looked up and there stood that Green Man. It scared them. Then Peg sed, "He ain't very big."

Then Peg told Hal, they's a still close by. She could smell it. But she warn't shore where it were at. She got to lookin', and there were mash everywhere in small cans. She knowed what that were for. It were to throw them off the trail. But Peg jist knowed the still were close by.

They decided to look for the still, but didn't find nothin'. When they got back to camp, somebody done et their lunch. Hal jist laughed. That little Green Man done pulled one on them. It were like a cat and mouse game and the green man had the upper hand. They had plenty of food, so it didn't hurt nothin'.

Peg sed, "Let's go deeper in the swamp. I jist know that still's in there somewhere. We won't cook anythin' till we git back."

They stayed in the swamp all day till 'bout dark. When they got back, they were a fire goin' and a big pot of stew on the fire. Peg looked at Hal and sed, "What is goin' on?"

They tried the stew. It were good. It had squash in it, taters, tomatoes and some swamp cabbage. Whoever made it knowed how to cook.

They was 'fraid to leave camp. They next day, they made like they was leavin'. Then they doubled back and hid in the trees. They stayed there all day, but nobody come. Peg told Hal, "He knowed we was here."

They cooked supper and went to bed. "Bout 1 o'clock they heard the worst noise they ever heard. So they stayed awake the rest of the night. They'd had 'bout all they could take of this place. They knowed they's no boogers, or they hoped not. But they didn't know what'd happen next.

The next night 'bout dark, they seen that Green Man again. They knowed he must be crazy. Nobody does what he does.

Hal told Peg, "One more night. If'n we don't find no still, we're goin' home."

That night 'bout dark, up walked a man. He looked old. He sed, "My name is Lyden Green. I've lived near the swamp all my life, and I don't like people to come in here and leave their trash."

Peg looked at 'im. He were 'bout the size of the Green Man. She asked 'im, "Are you the Green Man?"

He sed, "No, but I've seen 'im."

Peg sed, "Is there a still in these woods?"

Lyden sed, "They was a still over by the Iron Bridge, but it blew up one night and killed the man runnin' it. It were my boy. I told 'im not to make shine, but he wouldn't listen. They say he's the Green Man, but I ain't shore 'bout that."

Hal sed, "Did y'all git my stuff?"

He sed, "No."

Peg looked at Hal and sed, "It's time for us to go home and leave them alone."

Peg's still not shore if'n there's a real Green Man, or if'n Lyden's the Green Man. What do y'all think?

Them Hardaway Boys

Them Hardaway boys ain't got nothin' to do with the Fussell bunch, but it needs to be told anyhow. Their mama is Mary Lee. One of them boys is Wade, and the other is Gordon. They live over on Long Swamp there, 'bout 10 miles from where the Fussell boys growed up. Their dad homesteaded it a year ago. It's jist south of Woody Wagners and north of Dorothy McCall.

They say even the snakes try to hide when them Hardaways come in the swamp, but most of the time they jist ride everybody's cows. They even ride Dorothy's hogs. When she sees them she hollers and tries to hit 'em with 'er broom. Sometimes she even gits one of 'em. They's jist full of it. Mary Lee done cleared one acre of land cuttin' switches to warm their britches.

They got them a small bobcat and thought it would be fun to put it in Dorothy's chicken pen. So they slipped down to the chicken pen, but she were lookin' out the window and seen 'em. She got 'er broom, slipped by the barn jist as they was goin' a put that bobcat in the pen.

She hit Gordon up the side of 'is head and that bobcat come alive in Wade's hand. It 'bout eat 'im up. When she swung that broom, that cat run. Wade run, but she got Gordon real good that time. He hollered and then he run! Dorothy were shakin' 'er broom at them. Then she went to see Mary Lee to tell 'er what 'er boys done. Mary Lee sed she would take care of it.

Their dad come in from work, and he could tell she were real mad, so he didn't say much. When them boys come in, she lit in on them with a switch. Their dad sed, "They's jist boys." So she cracked 'im up side of 'is head with the switch she had. He run for the front door. Gordon jumped out the window and Wade run out the back door. They all knowed not to go back in till she cooled down.

They slept in the barn that night. They knowed they wasn't goin' inside all night, even if'n they was hungry.

The next mornin' their dad walked inside. Mary Lee had breakfast ready. Then come the boys. They walked in, but didn't say nothin'. She looked at the whole bunch. They et breakfast. It were real good. They looked at their mother and told 'er they wouldn't do nothin' to Dorothy again. They could tell she were still mad. Then Mary Lee sed, "We're goin' to Dorothy's house and talk to 'er.

Gordon sed, "I shore hope she don't have 'er broom!" Mary Lee looked at 'im and he knowed he'd done sed the wrong thang. So he shut 'is mouth.

They went to Dorothy's. They didn't know what were gonna happen. Gordon looked at Wade and whispered, "Mama's gonna hold us while she beats us with that broom!"

But Mama told Dorothy, "These boys is gonna clean y'all's barn, put up the hay and look after your cows. If'n they don't work, y'all let me know. I'll put a switch on their behinds like they never had afore."

Then their mama left. Wade asked Gordon if'n they was gonna leave too. Gordon sed, "Y'all can leave if'n y'all wanna, but I'm gonna stay here."

They shoveled all the cow manure out of the barn. It weren't bad work and they made fun out of it. 'Bout noon Dorothy told 'em that lunch were ready and to get washed up. She sed a prayer askin' the Lord to help. The boys guessed they needed it. She had a good lunch and they et it all. Then she told 'em to lay on the porch and rest some. In jist a little bit she sed they should go back to work.

It were gettin' late. Dorothy sed it were time to stop. She looked at the barn and sed it looked good.

As the boys walked home, Wade sed, "She's a nice person, even if'n she done swing a broom up the side of y'all's head." They both laughed.

They et supper, washed their face, washed their feet, laid down and afore they knowed it, it were day light. Their dad sed, "Git up. Time to go to work!" But they didn't go to Dorothy's house. They went straight to the barn.

When they had most of the barn cleaned, they fixed some of the gates. It really were fun to do what she didn't tell 'em to do. They put new boards where they was needed. Dorothy got the wood from Mr. Wagner. And they found some red paint.

They et lunch, laid on the porch and went back to work. When it were gittin' dark they left. Wade told Gordon, "Let's paint 'er barn."

So the next day they started to paint 'er barn. It sure looked good when they finished. They looked at the house. It had some bad boards, so they replace them. They had red paint left over so they decided the next day they could paint the back side of the house.

The followin' day they started on the back side of the house. Dorothy walked out. They thought she were gonna go git 'er broom, but then she laughed and sed, "They shore will be able to see my house."

The chicken pen needed to be rebuilt. So the boys jist started all over with it and built a whole new one. Dorothy got all the stuff to build it with. The boys' dad helped set it up.

She wanted to know if'n they knowed how to worm cows. They didn't, but told 'er they'd put the cows in the pen. They couldn't make them open their mouths, so they got a small hose, put the hose in the cow's mouth and put the worm pill at the end. Wade put 'is mouth on the hose. The cow burped and Wade got the pill! Gordon laughed and sed, "I hope it kills y'all's worms."

Finally the boys asked Mr. Wagner how to worm a cow. He come over and showed 'em how to check the cow for screwworms. Them cows was jist fine. They checked their hoofs, but needed some help. So they went back to see Mr. Woody. He sent Bert over to help them.

Bert asked "What was y'all thinkin' when y'all was gonna put that bobcat in the chicken pen?"

They sed, "We was gonna see 'im catch a chicken. But then he run and we ain't seen 'im since." They all laughed.

The next day were Saturday. Mrs. Dorothy had them hook up the buggy. It were easy 'nuff to do. Then she told them to clean up and put on clean clothes. They did, but didn't put on no shoes. Shoes hurt their feet.

Dorothy told Gordon to take the reins and take them to town.

When they got to Inverness, they shore were a lot of people. Dorothy bought everyone a hot dog. They et it up. Then Dorothy sed, "Let's go to the picture show."

The boys told 'er they didn't have no money for the picture show. But she told them to jist come on. She bought them popcorn and they et a bunch. She put salt on it. It shore were good.

The picture show were fun. The man couldn't ride that buckin' horse, but Gordon sed, "I could ride it."

The show were over. They shore did like it. Dorothy sed, "Some day we will do this again."

Mrs. Dorothy bought 'er food to eat at home for the week. They loaded the buggy and Gordon took them back home. They thanked 'er for takin' them to Inverness and the picture show.

The boys walked home. Mary Lee met them at the door and sed, "Boys, y'all don't have to do nothin' else at Dorothy's house."

Wade looked at Gordon and Gordon sed, "We don't have all the work done. We're gonna finish it." They had the house painted all red. Dorothy bought some white paint and they wanted to trim the windows in white and the doors, too. It looked good when they was done.

The boys done work for Dorothy for almost 2 years. She were such a nice lady. She paid 'em for some of the work they done, and they saved it all. They had 180 dollars. They went back to Inverness. Mrs. Dorothy paid for the show and the popcorn.

When the show were over, she were goin' shoppin' again. The boys went to the Ford place to look at all the cars. They knowed they couldn't buy a new one, so they jist looked at used ones.

Then the owner come out and asked how much money the boys had. They sed, "180 dollars."

So he told them to come and look at what he had. The body were beat up, but he sed it run good. It were a Model A. It shore weren't no looker, but the windows would roll up, and y'all could crank it with the crank.

Wade sed, "How much is this one?"

The owner sed, "180 dollars."

Then Gordon sed, "We gotta have gas money. If'n we could buy it for 75 dollars, we would buy it. The man walked around it 'bout 3 times and sed, "Can't do it."

The boys started to leave and the owner sed, "How 'bout 90 dollars?"

But Wade looked at Gordon. Gorden sed, "No, all we can spend is 75."

Gordon sed to Wade, "Let's go."

Then the man sed, "Give me the 75 dollars and the car is y'all's. Do y'all know how to drive?"

Gordon sed, "No."

So the owner had one of 'is boys show them how to drive and how to start it. The owner sed they could pick it up the next day.

They took the buggy back to Mrs. Dorothy, but didn't tell 'er what they'd done.

They didn't sleep none all night. They told Mrs. Dorothy they had somethin' to do the next day. They walked to the Ford place. He had it filled with gas. Gordon got in the driver's seat, pushed both levers up on the steerin' wheel, took it out of gear, turned the key, mashed the starter button and it fired up. Whew doggie! It shore run good. He put it in gear number one and let out on the clutch. They chugged off down the road. When they got to goin' he pulled the right lever down, jist like the man told them.

Gordon were havin' a little trouble keepin' it in the road. When they come to the gate, he forgot to mash the clutch and drove right through the gate. When they stopped they had to fix the gate.

They got the gate fixed. He pushed the lever on the steerin' wheel, took it out of gear, turned the key. It started right up. They drove to Mrs. Dorothy's, mashed the clutch and turned off the key.

Mrs. Dorothy sed, "Take me for a ride." So they went all through it again. They was havin' fun.

She asked what they paid for it and they told 'er. She sed she'd give them that much money for it. Then the boys didn't know what to do, but let 'er do it. They taught 'er how to drive. She weren't good at it at all.

The next Saturday, they drove it to Inverness. It were faster than 'er horse. Dorothy seen the doctor in Inverness. They didn't think much of it. Then they drove back to Mrs. Dorothy's house, put the car in the barn and walked home.

The next day, they cleaned up around the house. It looked good. When lunch time come 'round, they didn't hear from Dorothy, so they went home and et some cold biskets and cane s'rup.

James Carlton Fussell

The boys asked Mary Lee, "Is somethin' wrong with Mrs. Dorothy? We ain't seen 'er today."

Mary Lee sed, "I'll go see."

When she opened Dorothy's door, there she were, settin' in a rockin' chair. She had passed away, and in 'er lap she had an envelope. Mary Lee looked at the paper, she done left everythin' to Wade and Gordon. She wrote a note to Gordon. She left 'im her broom.

They buried 'er in the back yard. Their dad made a casket and in the note she told them she loved them all.

Ruth

Ruth lived on the Withlacoochee River, the second bend past the big oak tree. She done raised 2 boys. Her husband left 'er in the middle of the night and she didn't know why. Her boys sed she worked 'im to death. Either he worked, or she wouldn't feed 'im. Guess he got tired of workin' and jist up and left.

Ruth were a good lookin' woman. Now, they was a Yankee come to Inverness. When he seen 'er he perked right up. He started goin' out with 'er and in 'bout 2 months they got married. Ruth owned 'bout 10 acres of land, and she talked 'im into buyin' 10 more acres on the river.

Thangs seemed to be goin' good. Then he showed up with a knot on the side of 'is head. Someone asked one of Ruth's boys what happened to 'im. Her boy sed, "My mama told 'im to git up and he told 'er he'd git up when he were good 'n ready. So she hit 'im up the side of 'is head. And he got up."

She worked 'im real hard 7 days a week and if'n he didn't work, he had to sleep in the barn with no supper. Then one night he left. Ruth didn't know where he went.

In 'bout 3 months, she got her a new Yankee boy friend. He wined and dined 'er and in 'bout 6 months she married 'im. She talked 'im into buyin' 14 acres of land. That give them a good sized ranch.

One mornin' Ruth's boys told 'er they was goin' to leave and go somewhere for a while. They's never been anywhere. Ruth told them it were alright with 'her. And they left that mornin'.

James Carlton Fussell

Her new husband warn't much of a worker. He liked to lay 'round the house. Well, everybody knowed that warn't gonna work. He come to Inverness on a Saturday with a black eye, and told everyone he fell down. They all knowed what had done it, that fist of Ruth's and he warn't havin' fun at Ruth's.

When they got ready to go home from Inverness, he told 'er he were gonna sell the land he bought. But that night, Ruth told the law that he never come home and sed, "I guess he left." People was shore leavin' a lot. He didn't even take 'is clothes or whatever he had.

Ruth acted like she was heart broken, but people was beginnin' to think maybe she were a puttin' them husbands in the ground.

Ruth hired Ralph to help 'er with the ranch. He were a very humble man and he worked real hard. He warn't what y'all'd say were a good-lookin' man, and he didn't take no bath often. His teeth was bad, but everybody seemed to like 'im. Everybody has some faults.

Ralph slept in the barn and Ruth fed 'im real good, so he worked real hard.

Then one day the law come out to the ranch. They was checkin' on the men that done left. They looked all 'round and they seen a place that looked like somethin' had been buried there.

They didn't say much for 'bout 3 months. Ruth bought Ralph some new clothes and shoes. She made 'im take a bath once a week; that's 'bout what everybody done. Most people was happy for 'im.

When the law seen Ruth the next time, they told 'er they was gonna dig where she had buried somethin'. So the next week, they come to Ruth's house with some help. They dug where they thought somethin' were buried.

Ralph walked up where they was diggin'. The boys was back, and one of 'em sed, "That's where we..." But 'is brother told 'im to be quiet.

He sed, "Ok."

They dug down 'bout 3 feet and dug up some rib bones. They jist knowed they had done caught Ruth. She done kilt them men and buried them!!

They sent the ribs to Tampa to see if'n they was human. It takes 'bout a month to find out. The boys thought it were funny.

Then Ruth told her boys she were gonna marry Ralph. He were a good man. Most people thought it would never last, but it did.

In 'bout a month, they got the test on the rib bones back. It were deer ribs! Ruth laughed. She knowed it were deer ribs.

The sheriff warn't happy with Ruth and told 'er she shoulda told 'im it were deer ribs.

She sed, "Y'all didn't ask me."

The boys was laughin' and the lawmen didn't like it a bit. They covered the hole back up and left.

Ruth's boys was walkin' to the barn. One sed, "They was diggin' in the wrong place." And they both laughed.

Ruth and Ralph lived out their lives together livin' on the Withlacoochee River. Ruth's boys sold the land and house. They sold the cows, too, and moved to Tampa.

Did the law dig in the wrong place? Y'all can't ask Ruth and 'er boys won't tell.

James Carlton Fussell

Poems
by Red

James Carlton Fussell

That Red-Bone Hound

While travelin' through a small Georgia town,
It didn't have much, jist a little turn-a-round
Then an ole man walked up;
His teeth was all gone; 'is hair all gray.
Then he sed, "That's the meanest dog that's ever been in this town.
He bit the mailman, he bit the police, he bit a judge, the lawyers and
two doctors,
Jist 'bout every man in this here town.

But he belonged to Miss Sesslee. She's 93.
We all loved 'er, so we let 'im hang 'round.
Then one day we heard a lot of noise at Miss Sesslee's.
Two crooks tried to rob Miss Sesslee
But that red-bone hound put 'em up a Sycamore tree.

We all looked at 'em up the tree.
It were a sight to see.
The law come and took 'em down.
They sed, "Let's give them to the ole hound."
Everyone laughed, even that red-bone hound.

The next week we heard an awful sound.
It sounded like that red-bone hound.
We all run from down town
And there lay Miss Sesslee on the ground,
Next to that ole red-bone hound.

She passed away that day.
She loved that ole hound.
They buried Miss Sesslee the next day.
That red-bone hound set by 'er grave.
This were not 'is day while the preacher preached away.
Then the red-bone hound jist walked away.

The Mullet Boys

He left this town and a new family moved in.
They had a little girl that were jist three
She were deaf and played by the Sycamore tree.
But guess what walked down the street –
That ole red-bone hound.

We hope he don't hang around.
That girl of three played with that ole hound 'round the Sycamore tree.
Now, Mr. Brown were comin' to town.
The gate were left open, but not by that red-bone hound.

Out walked that girl of three.
She didn't hear a sound as Mr. Brown were comin' to town.
She walked in front of Mr. Brown.
But, that ole hound knocked 'er out of the way of Mr. Brown.

He run over that red-bone hound.
We all run down where Mr. Brown run over that hound.
Then Mr. Brown sed, "I didn't mean to run over that hound."
Now they's a monument to that ole red-bone hound.
The meanest dog in this here ole town.

James Carlton Fussell

Bill

There once were a man named Bill
He lived in Center Hill.
He made money with 'is still.
And stole chickens from Will
By 'is still.

Will shot Bill at 'is still.
Will told Bill,
"Next time I'll shoot your still
In Center Hill."

Then Will told Bill,
"I'll shoot you and the still,
Bill, on the hill in Center Hill
And there'll be no more
Bill in Center Hill."

The Mullet Boys

Billy

Billy in one of his nice new jackets
Fell in the fire and was burnt to ashes.
And now, although the room grows chilly,
I haven't the heart to poke poor Billy.

-Steve Fussell, Red's Nephew

James Carlton Fussell

Cooter Jones Died Today

I was settin' in the swing when up walked an ole man with a box
His hair had turned gray and 'is teeth was all gone
He sed, "My name's Cooter Jones
I'm jist passin' through.
I ain't had nothin' to eat in a day or two,
If 'n you could spare jist a little somethin' to eat
I'll tell my story to you.
I give 'im a big bowl of soup,
2 of them cat-eyed biskits
And a big glass of tea.

Then he sed, "I had family jist like you.
I went to Viet Nam in 1963
I crawled in them fox holes.
The captain thought a lot of me.
I was wounded, too.
They give me a purple heart.
They sent me home.
I married my sweetheart
She loved me.

I went back to Viet Nam
And crawled in them fox holes jist like before.
They shot me and I thought I were gone.
I were jist in my prime.
But it warn't my time.
I crawled out jist in time.
They give me that purple heart;
The captain pinned it on me.

I come back home, no more in Rome.
I got a new home.
Had 2 girls; I love them so.
I played a mean fiddle
And played with a big band.

The Mullet Boys

But I got into drugs and women,
I were jist all gone.
They couldn't depend on me.

I started back to Rome.
I don't have no home.
Nobody cares if'n I live or die."

I asked, "Where you goin' tonight, Cooter Jones?"
"Down by the creek.
They's an ole barn with some hay.
That's where I stay."
I sed, "I'll have somethin' for you to eat
If'n you stop by tomorrow."

The next day I looked
But no Cooter Jones.
Then I thought I should check the barn where he lay.

No more in Rome; he's found 'is home.
I called the sheriff and told where he lay.
They picked 'im up that very day.
They sed 'is heart jist give away.

They cremated 'im that day.
I returned home to swing that day.
Then I 'membered that box he had.
I'll bet it's in the hay.
I looked and there it were, right in the hay.

I opened it up and there were the medal,
Jist like he sed.
They give me 'is ashes today.
I spread 'em under the swing
So they wouldn't blow away.

Cooter Jones passed away today.

James Carlton Fussell

Recipes from Sally's Kitchen

Guava Pie

The hand-written recipes in the text were done by Red. Following are the same recipes in print.

James Carlton Fussell

Cracklin' Cornbread

½ c water ground cornmeal
2 Tbsp Sugar
3 Tbsp lard
½ c flour
1 egg
Milk enough to mix
1 c cracklin'
On hog killin' day, cook all the lard out of the hog skin.
Then squeeze out all the lard you can
Dry in the sun
Take a flour sack and put the skin in the sack
Beat it with a hammer till it's broke in small pieces
Mix with the cornbread
Bake for 20 minutes at 350 degrees

Pokeberry Leaves

¼ lb salt pork
1 ½ lb tender pokeberry leaves
3 qt cold water
Place salt pork in cold water
Bring to a boil, uncovered
Make sure you have only tender leaves
Bruise the leaves
Add to the pot and cook for an hour.
Add salt and pepper

James Carlton Fussell

Smoked Mullet

Don't take off the scales of the mullet
Fillet on the sides and take out the fins
Leave the back bone on one side
Salt and pepper
Make sure your smoker is hot
Put charcoal on the bottom with a pan of water above
Put the mullet fish side up, scale down side
Cook till they dry out some
Bigger fish take longer.
It's all 'bout the size of the mullet.

Facts About The Mullet Fish

Mullet ain't a very big fish, but y'all can find 'em all over Florida, along the coast in them rivers and 'round sandy beaches. They eat mostly green algae in there. But if'n y'all's gonna fish for 'em, you gotta use little tiny hooks and have lots of patience. They swim together in big schools and are real smart and fast. It's hard to catch them in clear water. Y'all can tell where they are 'cause they jump. That's how y'all know where to put y'all's hook in. These little mullet are good food for bigger fish too.

We used to seine fish, but it's illegal to fish with a seine now.

The mullet fish is an oily fish, so they smoke real good. They's 1 to 3 pounds each usually, but can git bigger'n 10 pounds.

Guava Pie

3 Tbsp flour
½ c sugar
1 lime, grated
1 tsp cinnamon
¼ tsp nutmeg
1/8 tsp salt
Graham cracker pie crust
4 c peeled, seeded and thinly sliced guavas
1 Tbsp lime juice
3 tsp cold butter cut in pieces

Set oven 425 degrees
Mix flour, sugar, grated lime, cinnamon, nutmeg and salt
Put guava slices on bottom of crust
Sprinkle with flour and sugar mix (can leave sugar out)
Sprinkle with lime juice and cut butter pieces
Lower oven temperature to 350 degrees
Bake 30-40 minutes

James Carlton Fussell

Sour Orange Pie

3 lg sour oranges
4 eggs separated
14 oz sweetened condensed milk
1 c whipping cream
Graham cracker crust

Heat oven to 350 degrees
Grate about half of the orange peel
Juice the oranges (no seeds)
2/3 c juice
Beat egg yolks, grated peel, juice and milk
Pour in crust
Bake 15-20 minutes or until it's thickened
Cool
Whipped cream for top of pie

Leaf from a Sour Orange Tree

Leaf from a Sweet Orange Tree

Glossary of Terms

Carpet Bagger - Northerners who came south with big long bags made of carpet. They would enter the homes of the southerners and jist take what they wanted.

Cat-eyed Biskits – Great big homemade biskits.

Chum – Bait for attractin' fish. Strong-smellin' fish scraps attract the fish. Shark works real well.

Blind – Hidin' place away from mosquitos while watchin' for animal activity in the area

Double Tide - Durin' a hurricane when the wind blows so hard and so long that the tide comes in and the wind holds it in. Then the next tide comes in right behind it causin' deep water on land.

Ice House - A small insulated buildin' on a dock to keep fish cold and fresh 'til sent to market. Blocks of ice were stored in sawdust 'til needed for keepin' fish that came in off the boats.

James Carlton Fussell

Rabbit Tobacco – A tall, wild plant dried and smoked as a substitute for tobacco. Parents encouraged their teenagers that if'n they was gonna smoke, to smoke rabbit tobacco. (It is actually good for lungs and sinus and has a slight sedative affect.)

Wild Rabbit Tobacco

Dried Rabbit Tobacco

Scabbard – A sheath for a blade or for a gun.

Seine – A method of river fishin' usin' a large net with weights on the

bottom edge. It hangs up and down in the water and traps fish when its ends are pulled together. This can be done by hand. Ocean seine fishin' is on a larger scale to catch bigger fish from big boats.

Skeeters – Slang for mosquitos

Snake – To move or twist. To get the big timber out of the swamp they had to hook chains around the fallen timber and "snake" it out by mule or horses to get it to the sawmill.

Sow Belly – Fat salt pork taken from the belly of a hog. The mostly white part of the bacon.

State's Evidence – To tell all about the crime, even against the others. Crooks used this to get a lesser penalty.

Sweetgum Ball: The prickly cones from a Sweetgum tree. They was often used for Christmas Tree decorations.

James Carlton Fussell

Album

*Red at two years old
with big brother
Lewis, Jr.*

*Big brother Lewis, Jr.
and Red at five years old.*

The Mullet Boys

Red's dad, Lewis Sr.

Red in school picture

Epilogue

My name is Red Fussell. I've been Red most of my life. I even sign checks and titles that way. That's all most people know me by. I done wrote this here book for the Fussell family. We was all kind in some way. Some of us has been good, some has been bad, and some of us has jist been!

I lived in Okahumpka all my life. My brother asked me one time why I didn't leave this place. I jist told 'im I liked it here.

Part of this book is 'bout friends I've met along the way. They's better than gold. Y'all can't buy or sell or trade friends. If'n y'all need somethin', they'll be right there, jist like Ray sed, "Never be greedy!"

I want to thank all the people who let me use their names in this book, even though they didn't know what I was gonna say about them. And I could never have written this book without the help of two special people, Sandy Kruse and Ruth Williams. All I done is write down stuff on paper and these wonderful ladies done all the rest. They's the kind of friends I have.

Red